MW01713782

Storied Landscapes

Hawaiian Literature & Place

1999

Library of Congress Catalog Card Number: 98-091779
ISBN: 0-9623102-7-1

Kalamakū Press
1710 Punahou Street, Apt. 601
Honolulu, HI 96822

Printed in the United States of America.

Cover Photo: *'Ai ā Manō* / "Eat like a Shark" by Anne Kapulani Landgraf. Kāne'ohe Bay is a spawning ground for hammerhead sharks. The sharks in the foreground are dead, tangled in a fishing net. The cliffs in the background are Mo'o Kapu o Hāloa ("Sacred Section of Hāloa"); the highest peak is Kānehoalani ("Kāne, Heavenly Companion"), separating Kualoa ("Long Back") from Hakipu'u ("Broken Hill"). The small island to the right is Mokoli'i ("Little Lizard").

CONTENTS

. . . Hawai'i is a place of mysteries, especially for old-fashioned Hawaiians—in the days and nights are woven magical happenings, seen in cloud formations, gusts of wind, and patterns of waves. In these elements, people were inspired to talk, letting the long hours pass as they spun tales and shared wondrous stories of the old days"—J.D. Holt, "Rainbows Under Water," *Recollections*

Deepest appreciation to
Richard Hamasaki,
Rodney Morales,
Gail Harada,
and Paul Lyons
for reading earlier drafts of these essays.

Storied Landscapes

Hawaiian Literature & Place

Dennis Kawaharada

NOIO

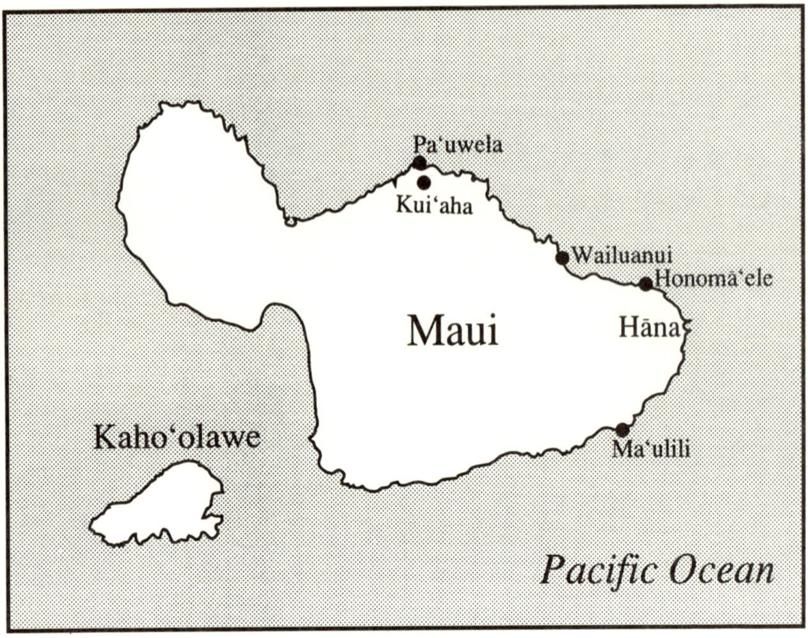
Pa'uwela
Kui'aha
Wailuanui
Honomā'ele
Maui
Hāna
Kaho'olawe
Ma'ulili
Pacific Ocean

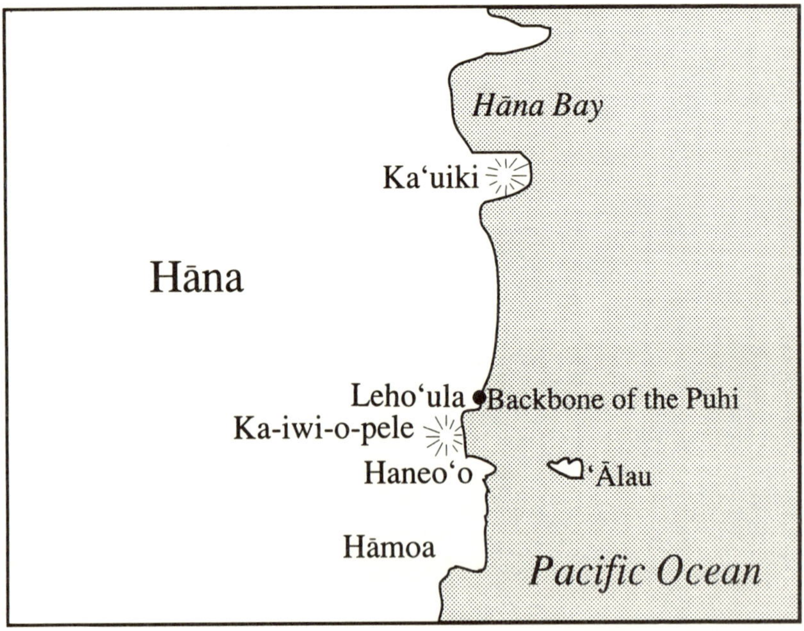
Hāna Bay
Ka'uiki
Hāna
Leho'ula
Backbone of the Puhi
Ka-iwi-o-pele
Haneo'o
'Ālau
Hāmoa
Pacific Ocean

A Search for Kū'ula-kai

Hāna, on the east tip of Maui, is famous for its low sky (Laniha'aha'a) created by clouds borne on easterly winds, gathering on the slopes of Haleakalā. Standing on Ka'uiki, the hill above Hāna Bay, the demi-god Maui pushed the sky up to make room for human activities. This steep-sided hill, rather small in reality (400 feet high) looms huge in the imagination:

> Shooting up to heaven is Ka'uiki,
> Below is the cluster of islands,
> In the sea they are gathered up,
> O Ka'uiki,
> O Ka'uiki, mountain bending over,
> Loosened, almost falling, Ka'uiki—ē.
>
> (Beckwith *Laieikawai* 340)

Atop this hill the prophet Hulumaniani built a heiau and prayed to his Akua to reveal to him the location of the princess Lā'ieikawai. Hāna was also known as the home of 'Aikanaka, an ancestor of the ruling chiefs of the Big Island of Hawai'i, and his wife Hinaikamalama, who leaped to the moon from a hill in Hāna to escape the unpleasant task of disposing of her child's excrement. Later, Hāna was the site of a battle fought by the Maui chiefs against 'Umi, an invading chief from the Big Island, who had crossed the 'Alenuihāhā Channel in a fleet of canoes; and around the fortified hill of Ka'uiki, battles between the warriors of Hawai'i and Maui were waged "for more than half a century" (Beckwith *Laieikawai* 339).

During my childhood in the 50's and early 60's, my family visited Hāna once a summer. At that time, I knew nothing about the traditional history of Hāna. Hāna was just a small town, a day-long excursion for fun from my grandmother's house in Kui'aha, a small pineapple plantation town on Maui's north shore.

My paternal grandparents, descendants of farmers from Hirōshima Prefecture in Japan, had immigrated to Hawai'i in the early 20th century; after saving his money, my grandfather bought some land in Kui'aha in 1929 and he and his wife opened a restaurant to serve breakfast and lunch to workers from the Pa'uwela Pineapple Cannery across the road. My father grew up in the house beneath the restaurant overlooking Kui'aha

Gulch, where my grandparents had planted mango, avocado lichee, and banana trees and raised ducks and pigs to support a family of ten children. In the early 50's, my father and mother, a Nisei from Hilo, settled in Kāne'ohe, O'ahu, where I grew up, one of three children. Once a summer we visited my grandmother on Maui.

To get to Hāna from Kui'aha, we took the "Hāna Highway," a narrow coastal road which cuts across pasture lands, then winds into gulches and out around headlands. On one side, smelling freshly green from early morning showers, a tropical forest slopes upward toward the two-mile high volcanic dome of Haleakalā; on the other side, brilliantly blue in the high summer sun, the Pacific Ocean widens to the horizon. We stopped to pick 'ōhi'a 'ai, juicy mountain apples, which ripen along the roadside in July and August; we swam in the mountain pools fed by streams and waterfalls flowing through the wettest terrain on Maui. One summer, one of the nearly dry streams was swarming with 'ōpae (freshwater shrimp) so many in the shallow water, we could scoop them up with our hands.

What brought me back to Hāna in 1991, two decades after my last visit, was the story of the Hawaiian fishing god Kū'ula-kai, given to me by a friend, Esther Mo'okini, a Hawaiian language teacher and translator of Hawaiian literature. The story was written down by Moke Manu, a native of Hāna; translated into English by Moses K. Nakuina; and published in Thrum's *Hawaiian Annual* in 1901 (reprinted in Manu 1-44).

Set in Hāna, the story tells how a fisherman became deified as the god Kū'ula-kai because of his mana in attracting and catching fish. Kū'ula-kai, "Red Kū of the sea," was married to Hina-puku-i'a, "Hina gathering seafood." The couple represents the male-female division of work in the kai, or sea: the husband fished from a canoe while the wife gathered seafood along the shore and on the reef flats. The god Kū, one of the four major Hawaiian gods, embodies the male energy of the universe; his name means "to stand erect"; he is balanced with a goddess, Hina ("to recline"), who represents the female energy.

Kū'ula-kai's brother, Kū'ula-uka ("Red Kū of the uplands") was a farmer. He was married to Hinaulu'ōhi'a ("Hina of the 'ōhi'a growth"), a deity of the forest and canoe-building. This couple represents the work of "uka," or the uplands. The Kū'ula brothers and their Hina wives, balancing uka and kai, land and sea, produced the necessities of life for the local community:

	Sea	Land
to erect	Kū'ula-kai	Kū'ula-uka
to recline	Hina-puku-i'a	Hinaulu'ōhi'a

After placing Kū'ula-kai in this mythological context, the story describes a rite of passage for Kū'ula-kai's son 'Ai'ai. One day a giant puhi (eel) named Koona came to Hāna and began stealing fish from the pond Kū'ula-kai had built to feed the ali'i of Hāna and the community. Kū'ula-kai and Hina decided to give their son the task of killing the puhi.

This puhi was a famous god of the north coast of Moloka'i, a worthy opponent against which to prove the mana of 'Ai'ai. One story tells of the puhi's battle with a giant manō (shark) who had become an outcast for eating his two younger brothers. Cannibalism was abhorrent to the Hawaiian gods and, to punish the manō, the people of Moloka'i were told not to feed him. Homeless and starving, he eventually invaded the puhi's sea cave. The puhi fought with and killed the manō. The cave, called Anapuhi, "Eel cave," is located in the cliffs just west of Hā'upu (Summers *Molokai* 184-185).

The puhi eventually moved to a cave called Kapukaulua ("The ulua hole"), offshore of Hāna, near the island of 'Ālau, from where he began raiding Kū'ula-kai's fishpond.

'Ai'ai located the puhi in its cave offshore, hooked it, and had the people of Hāna drag it ashore at Leho'ula, where he slew it with lava stones. With this deed, 'Ai'ai revealed that he had the mana to carry on his father's work. The backbone of the puhi, about 30 feet long, became petrified in the lava flats along the shore, where it remains—a monument to his heroic feat.

The kahu (caretaker) of the puhi then arrived from Moloka'i to avenge the death of his god. He told the chief of Hāna: "Your head fisherman [Kū'ula] told me to tell you that your head should be cut off and cooked in the imu, and the flesh of your body should be cut up and salted and dried in the sun." Enraged by the alleged insult, the gullible chief ordered his people to burn down Kū'ula's house, with Kū'ula and his wife and son in it. As the house burned, a wind from the sea blew the flames back at the people who set the fire, killing all of them, including the puhi's caretaker. Then Kū'ula-kai and his wife left their bodily forms and entered the sea as spirits, from where they control the comings and goings of fish. They took with them all fish from the seas of Hāna to punish the ali'i for his attack.

Like most traditional Hawaiian tales, the story ends with the triumph of the gods and the punishment of their enemies. 'Ai'ai escaped the burning house on a trail of smoke and entered a cave on Kaiwiopele Hill. He was befriended by a boy and, because of the kindness shown to him by the boy's family, 'Ai'ai called on his parents to bring back the hīnālea to the waters of Hāna. The ali'i who ordered the attack on Kū'ula's family met a fitting end: he choked to death on a hīnālea sent to him from 'Ai'ai's first catch.

I was interested in such fishing traditions because my father, who died in 1971 when I was 20, had been both a fisherman and a boat-builder. He built three boats, the last one 30-feet long, with an inboard diesel engine. He had a boat slip at He'eia Kea Pier in Kāne'ohe Bay and on weekends, went trolling for aku, 'ahi, ono, and mahimahi and bottom fishing for hapu'u, weke'ula, moano, and various kinds of snappers—'ōpakapaka, 'ula'ula, and uku. One of my earliest memories was night fishing on the bay by gas lantern light. I fell asleep in the cabin of our 22-foot boat anchored in the lagoon, off the edge of a reef, gently rocking, wavelets lapping against the sides. As I grew older, he took me farther out. At a spot for moano just inside of Moku Manu Island, he cut the engine and as we bobbed and drifted among the swells, we lowered lead-weighted hand-lines with multiple hooks into about 60 feet of water. I was amazed the first time I pulled up my line, and three reddish moano, about 8-9 inches long, were attached to it. Every so often my father would start the engine and move the boat back over the spot where the moano were biting.

At home, my mother dipped the fish in batter and fried them, the skin turning a crisp brown. The soft, flaky meat was 'ono:

'Ono, 'ono wale mai la no ka hoi ka i'a o ke kai
(Delicious, delicious—the fish of the sea)
A he moano kai lena, 'Ono! 'Ono!
(The moano of the yellowish sea, Delicious! Delicious!)

(Titcomb 110)

My father's youngest brother, Aki, told me he and my father had started fishing with their father along the north coast of Maui, at spots on both sides of Pa'uwela Point and Kui'aha Bay, which they called "Coconut Beach." Aki remembers: "Pop walked 2-6 miles from home to his favorite fishing holes—Lighthouse, Shark Hole, Coconut, Ma-ke Place, High Stone, Pandan Island, Straight, and Suda. The three boys liked to go to Coconut to poke fish. Pop enjoyed catching fish such as āholehole, mamo, menpachi ['u'u], pāpio, moi, po'opa'a, kūpīpī, moano." My aunt Hazel remembers that as a treat for his children on New Year's day, my grandfather presented them with "one āholehole each for good luck."

Years after my father's death, I wondered how he had gotten into building boats and deep sea fishing, how he had found the spot for moano in the "yellowish sea" (where the reefs starts dropping off into deep water) of Kāne'ohe Bay. Had someone told him about the spot, or did he find it by luck? He had the spot triangulated and could return to it whenever he wanted moano.

After a good day of fishing, he and his two friends would lay out a variety of colorful fish on the lawn; if there was a lot of small fish, some might be sold at Dote's Market or be given away to neighbors and friends. The big fish were divided up among the fishermen. Sometimes my mother would give me a sea bass to take to the family of my best friend, a Chinese-Portuguese boy who lived up Kea'ahala Road.

My father told my mother he wanted to retire from his job as a radio technician (he was only in his late 30's) and work as a fisherman; all she had to do was make enough money to pay the rent and buy rice.

The story of Kū'ula-kai evoked memories of my boyhood fishing trips with my father and our summer car rides to Hāna. It also raised some questions in my mind: where was Leho'ula? Were the petrified remains of the puhi slain by 'Ai'ai really there? Around this time, I began to be aware how little I knew about these islands that I called home. I had learned nothing about Hawaiian traditions during my colonial education in Hawai'i. In my 17 years of schooling in Hawai'i, including five years at the University of Hawai'i, not a single traditional Hawaiian story had been required reading. My teachers, many of whom, like my parents, were born and raised in Hawai'i and educated in the same public school and university system I had attended, spoke no Hawaiian and knew almost nothing about the 2,000-year-old traditions of the kanaka maoli—the first people to discover and settle the islands. The most famous place in Hāna was the Hasegawa General Store, established in 1910—as if history had begun there with the plantation era and the sale of consumer goods.

On our family trips to Hāna, we were third-generation tourists traveling through a tropical landscape, ignorant of the stories associated with the landscape, the record of human life from the preceding centuries. After a while, physical landscapes became boring, which is perhaps the reason I had not returned to Hāna in 20 years—the same hill, the same tree, the same fern, the same waterfall, the same road. Where were the spirits of the land? Was it possible to claim to know, to be a part of, to dwell comfortably in a place without honoring ancestral spirits and traditions which humanize every landscape?

The very idea of humanity required such an honoring; yet the Euroamerican colonial enterprise that had spread to all parts of the globe, including Hawai'i, had been disrespectful of indigenous peoples and traditions. The contempt toward natives was crystallized in such characters as the 17th century stereotype of Caliban in Shakespeare's play *The Tempest*. Subhuman, half-man, half-fish, a fool lusting after Prospero's daughter, Caliban represents the "Savage" that Europeans believed inhabited the Caribbean islands and other parts of the world. The notion of the superiority of Europeans and their culture has been perpetuated in British and American colonies through education, with its usually uncritical required readings of Shakespeare, Defoe, Kipling, London, and other writers who created patronizing or demeaning stereotypes of native peoples and societies. American missionaries and schoolteachers who came to Hawai'i attacked the native culture as "savage" and "pagan" and worked to suppress it. The Reverend Sheldon Dibble, a missionary-teacher at Lāhaināluna High School in the 1830's, who taught native scholars such as Malo and Kamakau, wrote:

> The Hawaiians were sorely oppressed, wretchedly destitute, and exceedingly ignorant; stupid to all that is lovely, grand, and awful in the works of God; low, naked, filthy, vile and sensual; covered with every abomination, stained with blood and black with crime. Idolatry also reigned with all its obscenity, frantic rage and horrid exhibitions of bleeding human sacrifices. (qtd. in Bushnell 16)

The *Pacific Commercial Advertiser* commented in 1862 on a project to take a hula exhibition to San Francisco: "A man must be pretty hard up for employment to undertake an exhibition of these islanders and their disgusting dances in a civilized country and a refined community" (qtd. in Noyes 38); in 1903, the missionary D.L Leonard boasted of "success" in the islands, "...a region larger than several of our states has been redeemed from utter savagery...the natives are steadily disappearing in number and seem likely sooner or later to disappear" (qtd. in Noyes 38).

More recently, in his essay "Marrakech" (1939), George Orwell sarcastically mimics the British-European attitude toward non-Europeans:

> When you walk through a town like this—two hundred thousand inhabitants, of whom at least twenty thousand own literally nothing except the rags they stand up in—when you see how the people live, and still more how easily they die, it is always difficult to believe that you are walking among human beings. All colonial empires are in reality founded upon that fact. The people have brown faces—besides, there are so many of them! Are they really the same flesh as yourself? Do they even have names? Or are they merely a kind of undifferentiated brown stuff, about as individual as bees or coral insects.

Later in the essay, Orwell refers to the "invisibility" of the native people. And American writer Joan Didion echoes his remarks 25 years later in an essay entitled "Notes of a Native Daughter": "...it is characteristic of Californians [of Euroamerican ancestry] to speak grandly of the past as if it had simultaneously begun, tabula rasa, and reached a happy ending on the day the wagons started west"—even though these settlers were crossing a landscape that had already been inhabited for 12,000 or more years. "Native" history, for Didion, is the five generations of her family living in the Sacramento area.

The story of Kū'ula-kai inspired me to revisit Hāna to see if I could find the sites associated with the traditions of this fishing god. It was a way to remember my father and to honor some ancient gods of Hawai'i. I wanted to look again at the places of my childhood with a different set of eyes, a different vision, based on a knowledge of stories that people the landscapes with ancient spirits.

I knew I would need the help of a kama'āina to find the backbone of the puhi. My friend Esther Mo'okini suggested I go and ask Clifford Hashimoto, the director of the Hāna Cultural Center, about the location of this legendary place..

On the way to Hāna, I stopped at Wailuanui, a site connected with the story of 'Ai'ai. At this bay, 'Ai'ai directed a friend in the capture of a giant he'e (octopus) using the famous cowry shell lure Leho'ula, bequeathed to 'Ai'ai by his father. This fishing expedition was a rite of passage for the friend, like the rite through which 'Ai'ai had passed in slaying the giant puhi that raided his father's fishpond. The he'e was attracted by the beautiful colors of the cowry shell and came out of its hole; when it rose to the surface on the shell, 'Ai'ai's protege shoved a stone into its head and being powerless to remove the stone, the he'e sank to the bottom and died. It was so large, only one arm could be transported back to Hāna aboard the canoes. The body and seven other legs were left in the Bay, where they turned to stones visible above the waves today.

On my childhood visits to Hāna, we had driven past the bay at Wailuanui without noticing it. This time I turned off the highway and followed the road down to the shore. Out among the waves, in the middle of the bay was a cluster of rocks: was this the remains of the he'e killed by 'Ai'ai's friend?

I found the Hāna Cultural Center in two small buildings on a slope overlooking Hāna Bay. I met the director in his office in an old one-room courthouse. He was part-Hawaiian, retired from military service. He had grown up in Hāmoa, an area south of Hāna town. We talked story a while and I told him about my grandmother's restaurant in Kui'aha, which he knew of. When I asked him about the Kū'ula-kai story, he said that while the natives of Hāna know the story, such old traditions were passing from living memory. When I asked him if the backbone of the puhi really existed, he said yes.

The conversation drifted into his family background. He told me his great-grandfather was one of the first Japanese plantation workers in Hawai'i in the 19th century. His grandfather worked on the coffee plantations on the Kona coast of the Big Island and married a Hawaiian woman; his father moved to Hāna. Coincidentally, *The Hāna News* (July 1991), which I found in my hotel room, carried an interview with

Hashimoto's sister reminiscing about growing up in Hāmoa. Her father, she said, "worked for the county. On the hillside by their home, he grew taro and planted sweet potatoes, cabbages, beans, pumpkin, squash and other vegetables for family use. ... Everyone worked and help out in the house or garden. At home, the Hashimoto children spoke English only; the adults spoke Hawaiian when they didn't want the children to know what they were talking about. Lani said her grandfather read Japanese newspapers, and translated the news into Hawaiian for his Hawaiian friends."

Hashimoto promised to show me the backbone of the puhi the next morning. I met him at 7:30 a.m., and after breakfast, we stopped at the Hāna Ranch office to get permission to cross their land. An office worker gave us the key to the gate blocking vehicle access to Leho'ula Beach, where the Ranch had a camping and picnic area. We drove across the pasture to the rocky beach. It was an overcast morning, and surf was breaking over the near-shore rocks. Hashimoto said that when he was young, he would walk along the coast past this area to school and that back then the remnants of a wall could be seen underwater, possibly the wall of a fishpond. No remnants were visible now. The shore formed a right angle, so a single straight wall could create an enclosure where schools of young fish might be trapped and raised. But the area was exposed to the prevailing trade wind swells and the big north swells of winter. Whether it had walls "twenty feet thick and ten feet high and an inlet for the fish to go in and out" (Beckwith 20) or was "a small rock-lined pool...principally for small fish" (Sterling 142), the fishpond would have been battered by waves and regularly maintained or rebuilt.

We walked along a narrow path through a thicket of hau trees and out to a stretch of volcanic rock near the breaking surf: there, in the lava, appeared a thirty-foot-long formation that looked like the backbone of a puhi. At that moment I was transported from modern Hawai'i into its ancient past: the spirits of Kū'ula-kai, Hina, and 'Ai'ai alive in the landscape. What a reader gains from a story like Kū'ula-kai's is knowledge, understanding, and appreciation of pre-Christian, pre-capitalist, pre-colonial Hawai'i and a closer connection to the land and sea. Like the many other stories from oral tradition recorded and published in Hawaiian or English during the 19th and 20th centuries (a literary tradition), the story of Kū'ula-kai contains history and geography, as well as religious beliefs and values that contributed to the survival and well-being of the kanaka maoli for over 80 generations.

***History*.** Kū'ula-kai's fishpond at the beach at Leho'ula must have been built at the beginning of the period of population expansion in Hawai'i, from 1100 to 1650 A.D. During this period, irrigation works, dry-land cultivation, and fishponds were developed and food production increased; at the same time, society became more stratified and ruling chiefs began to control larger areas of land (Kirch *Feathered Gods* 303-306). The chiefs became dependent on experts in fishing, farming, canoe building, and other arts to maintain their courts, make the land and sea productive, and feed the people. Experts of extraordinary talent were deified for their special mana and some (e.g.,. Kū'ula-kai, a fisherman; Kū'ula-uka, a farmer; Kūmokuhali'i, a canoe-builder) were given the name of Kū in honor of the war god whose mana had helped the ali'i conquer and control their domains. These experts were inventors of new, more efficient ways of doing things, builders of heiau, roads, extensive wet-land and dry-land plantations, fleets of voyaging and fishing canoes, and fishponds; they used the mana of Kū for peacetime activities.

Fishponds were constructed with two facing walls of stone or coral, filled with rubble. Ponds with walls 5,000 feet long (He'eia fishpond in Kāne'ohe Bay), 19 feet thick and 5.5 feet high have been documented (Summers *Hawaiian Fishponds* 5-6). Kamakau estimates that some of the fishponds would have required thousands of workers to build and maintain. Kikuchi believes that these large fishponds eventually served as status symbols for chiefs because they allowed the chiefs to enjoy "select fish on call" (299).

***Geography*.** Place names and the physical features and resources of each place were memorized in stories rather than recorded on maps or in books. The stories were geography lessons that familiarized the listener with the landscape they lived in. The numerous place names suggest a large population with a detailed knowledge of the islands; nuances of the landscape were noticed. Perhaps the most famous examples of such geography lessons are found in the story of the navigators Pāka'a and Kū-a-pāka'a. It contains wind chants naming dozens of ahupua'a (land sections) on each island and the winds associated with each—essential knowledge for sailing around the islands on canoes. (See Moses K. Nakuina's *The Wind Gourd of La'amaomao*.)

The story of Kū'ula-kai also contains dozens of place names, particularly those associated with ko'a, or fishing grounds. After his revenge against the king of Hāna was complete, 'Ai'ai is said to have dedicated his life to teaching the people of Hawai'i the arts of fishing and traveled from island to island locating or establishing places to gather sea resources on Maui, Kaho'olawe, Lāna'i, Moloka'i, O'ahu, Kaua'i and Hawai'i. For example, at Honomā'ele, Maui, he established a ko'a for 'āweoweo; at Polihua ("Bosom [of] eggs"), a beach on the northwest coast of Lāna'i, he placed a stone to attract honu ashore to lay their eggs; at a beach near Kaunakakai, Moloka'i, he discovered pua 'i'i (baby mullet) swarming near shore, and began a practice of kicking them onto the sand with one's feet; on the cliffs of Makapu'u, O'ahu, he placed a fishing stone called Mālei, to attract and multiply uhu, for which the sea below the cliffs is famous.

Religious Beliefs: The belief in the mana of stones to attract fish, even when the stones were placed on land, is based on the observation that fish congregate around rock and coral formations in the ocean to graze on limu growing on them or to hide in holes from predators. Mālei, the uhu stone of Makapu'u, is just one such fish-attracting stone. The first fish stone set up by 'Ai'ai, at Leho'ula, was called Pōhaku-mūone ("Sandstone"); another stone, called Kū-a-lanakila ("Stand in victory"), was set up at Hāmoa; a third at Kau'iki was called Makakiloi'a ("Eyes of the fish spotter").

Such stones have become the source of modern legends. One such fishstone, "formerly located in a place next to the fish pond of Haneo'o [in Hāna]," was taken home by a Japanese man named Murakami. He worshiped the stone by pouring sake (rice wine) on it, apparently hoping to "improve his luck in fishing":

> Many Hawaiians advised him that the stone would only cause trouble for him, but he disregarded this warning. Sometime after the "installation" his first son died in an accident; Hawaiians again remonstrated but their warnings were disregarded. After another period of time his second son became insane. (Sterling 150)

Finally, Murakami had the stone broken into pieces and thrown into an imu fire. (Burning in an imu was a traditional Hawaiian practice for destroying one's enemies.) A terrible stench is said to have permeated the land around the imu. The story does not make it clear whether Murakami's family was punished by the Christian god for worshipping a "pagan" stone; or by the Hawaiian gods, for moving the stone from its original place or inventing an inappropriate rite of worship.

Mālei, the uhu stone of Makapu'u, also figures in misfortunes. It is said to have been thrown into the sea, buried, or broken up by the haole keeper of the Makapu'u lighthouse, who was told the stone was causing the illness of his Hawaiian wife; he himself died soon after getting rid of the stone (Sterling and Summers 258-259).

In traditional times these fish stones were sites of worship where the first fish caught were placed as offerings to give thanks to the gods and insure a future supply—one fish for the male (Kū) and one for the female (Hina). 'Ai'ai is said to have spread this practice throughout the island as a form of worshipping his father and mother, and his work made them the chief fishing gods of Hawai'i.

These altars were constructed by placing a single special stone or groups of stones or a piece of wood inside a ring of smaller stones; or by piling up stones and coral into a mound. Such constructions were found throughout the islands along the coast. The piles of stones and coral seem to imitate the ko'a, or coral mounds in the sea where fish congregate; these altars are called by the same name, ko'a, or ko'a kū'ula, or simply kū'ula; however, not all ko'a were erected for Kū'ula-kai. Kamakau notes that Kū'ula, "a great fisherman of ancient times," was "the main 'aumakua of fishermen," but there "were a great many fishing 'aumākua, each related to his descendants, and each raised above [all others] by his own descendants" (*Works* 61).

A ko'a could be dedicated to any of the fishing gods: "The people whose god was Kū'ula built Kū'ula ko'a; those whose god was Kānemakua built Kānemakua ko'a, and those of Kinilau, Kamohoali'i and Kāneko'a did likewise, and so there were many, many ko'a" (*Works* 133). Traditions of fishing gods besides Kū'ula-kai have been passed down: Maikohā (the god who transformed himself into a wauke plant, from whose bark kapa is made) had four sisters who are said to have transformed themselves into fishing spots or fishponds around O'ahu: the sister Kaihuopala'ai became a fishpond for 'anae at Kapapaapuhi in 'Ewa; the sister Kaihuko'a changed into a fishing ground near Ka'ena, where ulua, kāhala, and mahimahi are caught. Ihukoko, a third sister, went to Kawailoa in Waialua, bringing āholehole with her; and Kaihuku'una ("ku'una" is a place where a fishing net was lowered and set) went to Lai'e in Ko'olauloa, bringing 'anae to the area. Their oldest brother, Kāne'aukai ("Kāne, the ocean traveler") floated ashore as a piece of wood at Mokulē'ia and became a fishing god for the North Shore of O'ahu. (Fish are attracted to things that float at sea, like pieces of wood—small fish for food or protection from birds, bigger fish to feed on the small fish.) A ko'a was set up for Kāne'aukai at Keahuohapu'u, the bluff on the south side of Waimea Bay dividing the district of Waialua from Ko'olauloa; the ko'a is said to attract 'anae and kala, which are abundant in the area from April to July (Fornander, Vol. 5, 270-273).

Ethics: The story of Kū'ula-kai is primarily a religious text. Kū'ula-kai and 'Ai'ai, like other gods, established good practices and exemplify values. One such value is to work to benefit the people. Kū'ula-kai is remembered for constructing the first fishpond to feed the chief and people of Hāna; 'Ai'ai for teaching the arts of fishing and locating and establishing fishing grounds throughout the islands.

'Ai'ai also encouraged generosity. At Ma'ulili Bay on Maui, when a stranger named Kānemakua ("Kāne, the parent," a fishing god) drifted by in a canoe, without a fish, 'Ai'ai gave him the first fish caught at the fishing ground, advising him to share whatever he caught with others and so become known for generosity. The traditional culture encouraged people to take care of not just themselves or their relatives, but guests and strangers as well. Stinginess and greed were punished; chiefs and others who did not distribute the wealth of the land and sea fairly were deposed or killed. One story tells of how the fishermen of Ka'ū were angered by the greed of their ali'i, who always wanted to keep the entire catch of aku for himself. They loaded down his canoe at sea with fish so that it swamped, then left him to drown (Pukui *Folktales* 74-75). (The so-called "Aloha Spirit" represents the tourism industry's commercialization of this tradition of generosity and hospitality, whose original purpose was to create community, not profit.)

The distribution of the catch became formalized to insure that everyone got a fair share. For example, the first day's catch of kala (unicorn fish), taken with hīna'i (basket traps), was given to the chief, who gave 20-40 fish from each trap to the akua; from these, 3-5 from each trap went to the fisherman. On the second day the catch from the first trap pulled up was cooked and offered to the fishing 'aumakua, after which the fish was free to be eaten by the fishermen and the heads of households. Then an offering was made to the female 'aumakua and divided among the households living in the ahupua'a (Kamakau *Works* 85).

'Ai'ai also taught conservation of fish and other sealife. At Wailau on Moloka'i, he witnessed "wanton" overfishing of 'o'opu and 'ōpae "without any thought of conservation for their propagation," so he punished the people by making the 'o'opu and 'ōpae disappear: "those in the water went up the stream to a place called Koki, while those in the gourds were turned into lizards which scampered away"(Manu 22-23). The practice of conservation was commonplace and widespread in traditional Hawai'i. The rule was to take only what you needed and in such a way that whatever was gathered would regenerate by the following season (e.g., breaking off the branches of seaweed rather than uprooting the plant; not taking female fish during spawning season). The konohiki, or overseer, of an ahupua'a was responsible for examining the condition of plant and animal life on the reefs. He could place a kapu on any form of life that needed protection (Titcomb 14). A person who broke a kapu could be punished or put to death—by a chief or a god. At Paumalū ("Taken secretly"), on the North Shore of O'ahu, a woman who tried to take more he'e than was permitted by the ali'i and his konohiki had her legs bitten off by the guardian manō of the area (McAllister 151). (Recently, a diver spear-fishing at night near this same area was bitten by a shark.)

The basis of this conservation of resources was the rootedness of the people in the 'āina and kai; an 'ohana (extended family) lived for generations in the same place. They were nourished by the land and sea where they lived, directly accessing the food supply. The ideal was to protect the life of the land and sea for their descendants, in perpetuity; each generation was responsible for ensuring the food supply for future generations. The limits of resources on their small, isolated islands were clear; they could see the boundaries of the ahupua'a that fed them, from this mountain ridge to that mountain ridge, and within these boundaries was everything they needed for their survival and well-being. The 'ohana were in daily contact with the environment and could observe the effects of their activities on the plant and animal life. When fish were less abundant or schools of migratory fish were late in arriving, there must have been anxieties about the possibility of hunger or famine. The response was both practical (limits on the taking of fish) and religious (the worship of gods who could attract fish). Today, with most of our food and other needs imported, conserving island resources is not as obvious a need, or as high a priority, as it was in former times.

When my father brought home our first RCA black-and-white television in the 50's, the images, music, and messages of modern American culture flowed continually into our living room, promoting youthful rebellion, individualism, and wasteful consumption of mass-produced food and disposable products. It was a culture created by capitalists whose mission was to exploit and profit from labor, resources, and markets on a global scale. Like the greedy eel who came to raid the fishpond of Kū'ula and Hina, capitalism broke into Hawai'i in the 19th century and disrupted the traditional economy and way of life. Television was just its latest tool for imposing its beliefs and values globally.

Capitalism detaches individuals from family and birthplace, offers jobs and livelihood to those willing to move where their labor or skills are needed. It draws the landless, the impoverished, the discontent, the refugee from home. Some of the factors in the disintegration of the 'ohana rooted in Ka'ū, Hawai'i, have been identified by Handy and Pukui:

> Partly as a consequence of the sudden abandonment of the kapu (legal tabu) system in 1819; partly due to the influence of foreign education imposing from the outset Euro-American principles, conceptions and ideals of marriage, relationship and duty: but chiefly as a secondary consequence of the marriage of Hawaiian women to white and Oriental men (often for the sake of economic security under the new system), the 'ohana system has lost its integrity....
>
> Along with the disintegration of the 'ohana and concurrent economic changes has gone the removal from 'āina or land of birth. When a Hawaiian woman married a man of another race it was not only likely to remove her and her children somewhat from the 'ohana, but also from the 'āina. Other influences, in Ka'ū as elsewhere, potent in separating individuals from homeland have been: in the early days the recruiting of native sailors for whaling; the establishment of the sugar plantations; ranching, which inevitably had the effect of

> disrupting native agriculture, the taking over of commercial fishing and favourable fishing localities by Orientals; the substitution of rice for taro in irrigated land (lo'i), and of Oriental for Hawaiian labour where taro continued to be grown; and last but by no means least the steady flow of Hawaiians to Honolulu, the able-bodied men seeking work on the waterfront, in the public services and government offices, both sexes being drawn thither for purposes of being taught and of teaching, elders coming to be with their young folks, and many lured from the country by the excitement, sociability, and conveniences of city life. (15-16)

Other factors in the disruption of the traditional way of life included foreign diseases, which decimated the Hawaiian population and made the 'ohana less functional; the conversion of land into private property (1848); the passage of a law allowing foreigners to buy and own land (1850), with a promise that it would attract foreign investment and bring wealth and prosperity to the islands by making possible the development of extensive ranches and plantations; the overthrow of the Hawaiian monarchy after it became an obstacle to foreign profiteers (1893); and five years later, the annexation of the islands by the United States (Kame'eleihiwa *Native Land* 137-318).

A familiar story. Capitalists, backed by the military forces of imperialist nations, have been roaming the globe for centuries, competing for and taking control of land and resources. When the opportunities for profits diminish in one place, they leave to seek their fortunes elsewhere—kōlea, as Pi'ilani calls them, birds that come to Hawai'i in the winter to get fat before flying off to their summer nesting grounds in Alaska.

The accumulation of capital has no limits—products are turned into money, which is stored in banks, invested, or spent. Driven by competitive greed and anxiety over not having enough, individuals exploit resources and reap profits beyond what they or their children would need or could spend in multiple lifetimes. The religions of capitalism preach that this world doesn't matter (so why conserve its resources?); only the spiritual hereafter counts. On the other hand, to be wealthy in this life, not to suffer any physical wants, to be better off than others are signs of God's love.

In 1989, a fleet of 13 long-line fishing boats owned by Vietnamese immigrants, refugees of a capitalist war, arrived in Hawai'i via Louisiana, where they had been catching shrimp (*Honolulu Advertiser* August 29 B1+). Long-liners lay several miles of line, with hundreds of hooks, catching indiscriminately whatever swims by and throwing away what can't be sold. They have been accused of decimating the world's populations of swordfish, tuna, and sharks. The immigrant fishermen, all belonging to one extended family, once rooted in an ancestral homeland, now rootless, came to Hawai'i because the weather was bad for half of the year in the Gulf of Mexico, and the competition for shrimp was fierce; they had heard that the weather was good in Hawai'i and profits could be made in long-line tuna fishing. One of them summarized their motivation: "If over here good, then stay here. If not good, go somewhere else. We just want to make money." After the fishermen encountered opposition to their rapacious method of fishing and discovered that they would have to give 10% of their profits to the local fishing auction agency (in the Hawaiian tradition of sharing a part of the catch with one's community), they were considering moving on to Guam, where "They got no rules, a lot of fish, not so many boats."

Local commercial fishermen, also profit-seeking, have overfished the waters of Hawai'i, depleting the very resource that is their livelihood. After the abandonment of the konohiki and kapu system in the early 19th century, there was no regulation of fishing. Unclaimed inshore fishing grounds and all the fishing grounds beyond the reef were opened to everyone by Kamehameha III. The stocks of near shore fish dwindled as population increased, fishing methods became more efficient, and more and more people fished without limits on their catch.

In the 1980's, the state and federal governments stepped in as modern konohiki and established conservation laws: controlling the number of commercial fishermen through licensing, limiting the size and number of fish taken, placing restrictions on types of equipment used, prohibiting fishing during spawning seasons or in designated areas, and so on. Still, local fishermen complain that fish and other seafood such as limu (seaweed) and 'opihi (a shellfish) are scarcer now than ever before. Recently, the catch of choice deep-sea bottomfish ('ōpakapaka, 'ula'ula, and uku) began decreasing dramatically around the major islands; and the state, supported by some worried commercial fishermen, is planning to restrict bottom fishing at designated fishing grounds during spawning season while doing research on how to re-build and maintain the stocks of these fish.

But governments have limited resources and personnel for enforcing their fishing laws. Today, conservation would work only if informed communities, rooted in place and committed to protecting resources for future generations, adopted restrictions on production and consumption, along with population and pollution controls. And such practices would have to be applied globally: fish stocks around the world have been "damaged by pollution, by destruction of wetlands that serve as nurseries and provide food, by the waste of unprofitable fish (called 'bycatch'), and, above all, simply by overfishing. As a result of these changes, some fish stocks have collapsed, and many important groups of fish are fished either to the sustainable capacity or beyond it" (Parfit 9). The United States and Canada have fished out Atlantic cod and redfish and are now debating sustainable salmon quotas in the Pacific Northwest. While national laws apply out to 200 nautical miles from terrestrial borders, the ocean beyond can be regulated only by international treaties. Fish in open waters are being scooped up by giant high-tech trawlers, factories at sea, backed by national governments: "The hungry, restless, distant-water ships of Spain, China, Russia, Poland, Japan, South Korea, Taiwan, and many others, forced from their traditional grounds by 200-mile limits or by stock declines at home, search the world" (Parfit 21).

As the high winds of greed sweep the fire of global capitalism from Europe and America across Asia, Africa, South America, and Oceania, consuming everything in its path, the ancient fishing gods may be forced to flee the burning planet, finding refuge elsewhere and taking all the fish in the seas with them.

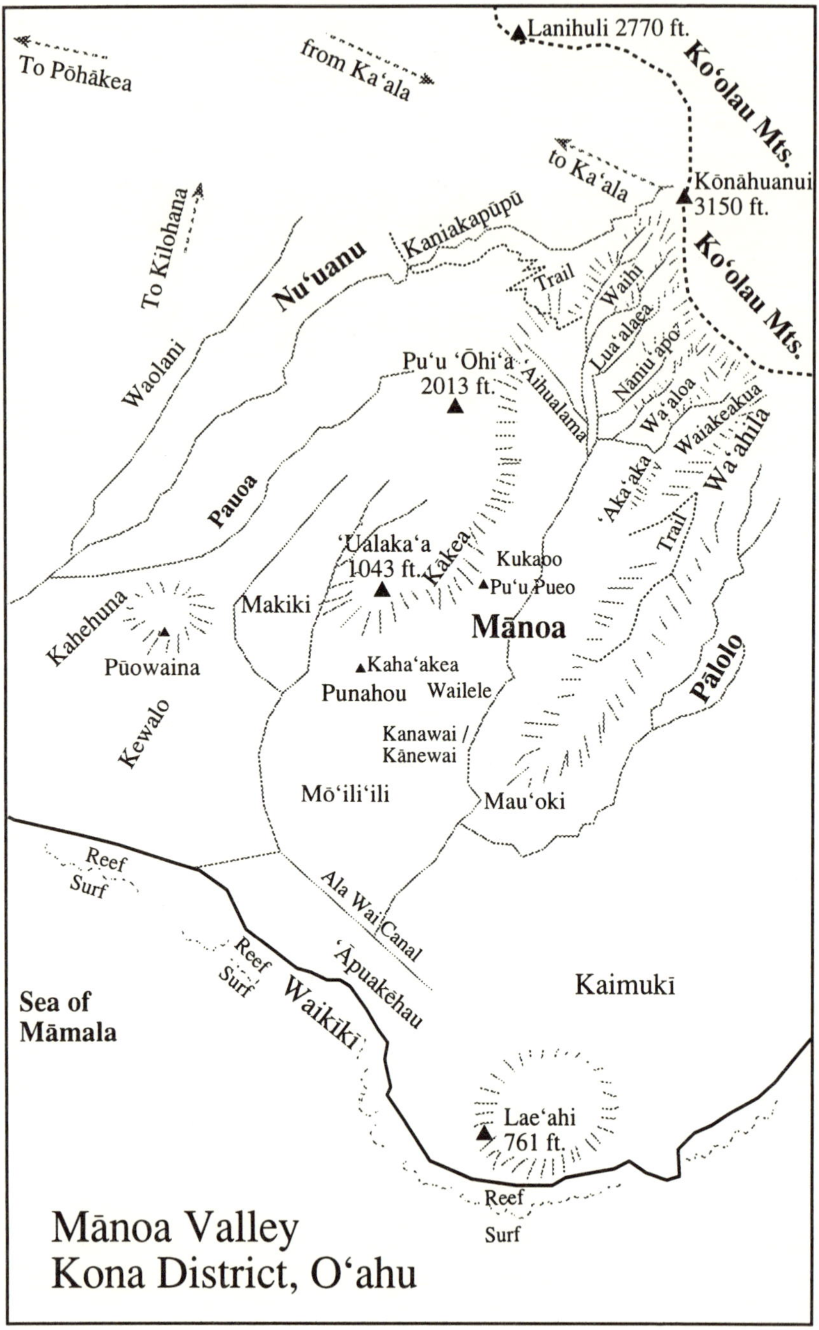
Lanihuli 2770 ft.
To Pōhākea
from Ka'ala
Ko'olau Mts.
to Ka'ala
Kōnāhuanui
3150 ft.
To Kilohana
Kaniakapūpū
Nu'uanu
Trail
Waihī
Ko'olau Mts.
Waolani
Lua'alaea
Pu'u 'Ōhi'a
2013 ft.
'Aihualama
Nāniu'apo
Wa'aloa
Waiakeakua
Wa'ahila
Pauoa
'Aka'aka
Trail
'Ualaka'a
1043 ft.
Kākea
Kukaoo
Pu'u Pueo
Makiki
Kahehuna
Mānoa
Pūowaina
Kaha'akea
Punahou
Wailele
Pālolo
Kewalo
Kanawai /
Kānewai
Mō'ili'ili
Mau'oki
Reef
Surf
Ala Wai Canal
Reef
Surf
'Āpuakēhau
Kaimukī
Sea of
Māmala
Waikīkī
Lae'ahi
761 ft.
Reef
Surf
Mānoa Valley
Kona District, O'ahu

ʻAumākua of Kona, Oʻahu

In 1979, I moved into a 6th-floor apartment at the foot of ʻUalakaʻa ("Rolling Sweet Potato"), a hill in Makiki at the border of Mānoa, in the Kona district of Oʻahu, which encompasses the city of Honolulu. Makiki is in a climatic transition zone between the cool, rainy Koʻolau mountains and valleys, and the hot, arid coastal plains. On most days, clouds form along the summit ridge of the Koʻolaus. When rain drifts down the valleys, and sunshine prevails along the coast, rainbows often appear, marking the boundary between wet and dry.

Makiki, named for a type of stone found here, is one of the most densely populated areas of Honolulu, with high-rise condominiums alternating with low apartment buildings along its narrow streets. Urban apartment living is about as far as you can get from the life of farming and fishing of ancient Hawaiʻi; one could live a lifetime in a concrete cubicle in Honolulu, commuting over asphalt roads and freeways to and from work at another cubicle; frequenting supermarkets, shopping malls, restaurants, bars, movie theaters, and sports arenas; or staring into the virtual reality of television and computer screens, linked electronically to America, Europe, and Asia—without any connection to the storied landscape outside.

1. Moʻo / Water Lizard

To the east of Makiki lies Mānoa ("Wide"), a U-shaped valley with six streams (Aihualama, Waihī, Luaʻalaea, Nāniuʻapo, Waʻaloa, and Waiakeakua) flowing down from the Koʻolaus into Mānoa Stream and out to sea at Waikīkī (since the 1920's, into the Ala Wai Canal). Today Mānoa is a middle-class residential district of mainly single family homes; in former times it was filled with loʻi (taro ponds): "In upper Mānoa, the whole of the level land in the valley bottom was developed in broad taro flats. The terraces extended along Mānoa Stream as far as there is a suitable land for irrigating" (Sterling and Summers 282).

Mānoa down to Mōʻiliʻili was known for its moʻo—water spirits, usually female, in the form of large lizards. Moʻo are ʻaumākua, or ancestral gods, who protect their descendants from danger or sorcery, heal sickness or wounds, and forgive transgressions; they can restore a person to life or guide the spirit of the dead to join the spirits of its ancestors in the afterworld: "O ke ola ia a ka ʻaumakua" ("Life from the ʻaumakua") is the saying (Kamakau *People* 28). The ʻaumakua can also be an avenger against one's enemies or against worshipers who break vows sworn in the name of the ʻaumakua "or who stupidly eat things consecrated to them, or which are the forms [of their ʻaumākua], or who eat defiled things; who break laws, commit adultery, and disregard the laws of God, of the land, of parents, husbands, wives, children, and relatives" (*People* 29). These spiritual beings take the visible bodies of natural elements (thunder, lightning, lava or volcanic fire), or animals, such as the pueo (owl), manō (shark), honu (turtle), puhi (eel), or moʻo.

The moʻo is black, between twelve and thirty feet long (Kamakau *People* 83). As no such large water lizards ever existed in Hawaiʻi, it may be an ancestral memory of the crocodiles or Komodo dragons of the Indonesian archipelago. Small skinks and geckos are considered by some to be kinolau, or bodies, of the moʻo (Handy and Pukui 125). Kamakau denies this, though he says "one can imagine the shape [of a moʻo] from these little creatures" (*People* 83). The ʻoʻopu, a lizard-looking fish that lives in streams and tide pools, is also considered by some to be a kinolau of the moʻo.

According to Beckwith, moʻo worship was brought to Hawaiʻi from Tahiti, where the moʻo was worshiped by the royal Oropaʻa family (*Hawaiian Mythology* 128). The moʻo migration came under the aliʻi Moʻo-i-nanea ("lizard-that-enjoys-itself") and landed first at Waialua, Oʻahu (Handy and Pukui 125). The ancestral moʻo goddesses were named Walinuʻu, Walimanoanoa, Kalamainuʻu, and Kihawahine (Kamakau *People* 85).

The rainy cliffs and mountain peaks, waterfalls, springs, streams, and pools of Mānoa were dwelling places for moʻo. A moʻo lived on Kōnāhuanui, the highest peak in the Koʻolaus, above the back of the valley (Summers and Sterling 312); the area around her home is the second rainiest on Oʻahu, averaging 150 inches per year. At Pūʻahuʻula ("Spring of the Red Feather Cape"), in upper Mānoa, the moʻo goddess Kihanuilūlūmoku lived; her water nourishes the plants of Waʻaloa ("Long Canoe"), the second stream from the east. Pali Luahine ("Luahine's Cliff"), on the east side above Woodlawn, was the home of Luahine, a moʻo who came from Maunalua Fishpond (Summers and Sterling 290). Mōʻiliʻili ("Lizard-pebbles," or "Lizard Piled-up"), on the coastal plain below the valley, is named for a giant moʻo slain by Pele's sister Hiʻiaka and turned into a long rocky hill. (Pukui et al, *Place Names*; Sterling and Summers 277-78; the hill, cut through by the H-1 Freeway, is across from Kūhiō School).

Moʻo were also guardians and caretakers of fishponds. On Oʻahu, Kanekuaʻana was the guardian of ʻEwa and the fishponds of Puʻuloa ("Long Hill," Pearl Harbor); she brought an abundance of pipi (oysters),

ʻōpae (shrimp), and nehu (anchovy). Laniwahine was the guardian of ʻUkoʻa fishpond in Waialua; Hauwahine guarded the ponds at Kawainui and Kaʻelepulu in Kailua, Koʻoluapoko; and Laukupu the pond at Maunalua, on the east end of Honolulu. "They were the guardians who brought the blessing of abundance of fish, and of health to the body, and who warded off illness and preserved the welfare of the family and their friends" (Kamakau *People* 84). When the chiefs or their agents abused the poor and the fatherless, the moʻo guardians took the fish away—until the wrongdoers showed penitence and made restitution to their victims (Kamakau *People* 85).

"Punahou," by Emma M. Nakuina, tells a tradition of the creation of Punahou Spring by a moʻo god named Kākea. (The story was published in Thrum's *Hawaiian Annual* in 1893 and reprinted in *Ancient Oʻahu* 45-50. The author was born in Mānoa in 1847, the daughter of Theophilus Metcalf, a sugar planter and government surveyor, and Kaili Kapuolono, an aliʻi; the well-known writer Moses K. Nakuina was her second husband.)

The main characters in "Punahou" are twin rain spirits: a boy named Kauawaʻahila (a rain of Nuʻuanu and Mānoa) and his sister Kauakiʻowao (a rain and fog carried on a cool mountain breeze). The twins were abused and neglected by an evil stepmother named Hawea while their father Kahaʻakea was away on Hawaiʻi Island. The siblings fled from their home near Mount Kaʻala, the highest peak on Oʻahu (4,020 ft.) to Kōnāhuanui above Mānoa. The affinity of the twins for mountain peaks suggests their rain cloud forms and also their moʻo ancestry; their flight from Kaʻala to Kōnāhuanui depicts the movement of rain clouds associated with cold fronts which sweep over the islands from west to east during the rainy season of Hoʻoilo (October to April).

Pursued by their mean-spirited stepmother, the twins fled from Kōnāhuanui to the head of Mānoa Valley. Like a cold north wind behind a passing front, Hawea followed her stepchildren to the head of the valley, so the twins went down the valley to Kukaoo Hill (where a heiau is located, at 2859 Mānoa Road); then to the rocky hill behind Punahou School. The movement of the twins down the valley represents the path of the rains called Kauawaʻahila and Kauakiʻowao sweeping from the wet uplands toward the dry plains. Each stop is drier than the last, with less food. At Kukaoo hill, the twins planted and ate sweet potatoes, a dry-land crop, not as prized as the wetland taro of the upper valley. At the rocky hill near the mouth of the valley, they lived on leaves, flowers, and fruits and on "grasshoppers and sometimes wild fowl." The rocky hill marks a rain boundary: it may be pouring rain in the upper valley, while it is sunny and dry below the hill.

At their home near the hill, the sister Kauaki'owao asked her brother Kauawa'ahila for a pool to bathe in. The brother went to a pond called Kanawai (perhaps Kānewai, near the mouth of Mānoa, said to be connected by an underground stream to the sea; see Sterling and Summers 281); there he called on the mo'o Kākea, a maternal ancestor, who "controlled all the water sources of Mānoa and Makiki Valleys." (Kākea is also the name of a bluff on the west side of Mānoa Valley, and the name of a stormy wind of Mānoa.) Kākea helped his grandson Kauawa'ahila by digging an underground tunnel from Kanawai to the rocky hill in Makiki to supply the pool of water his sister Kauaki'owao desired; the god also promised to ensure the supply by diverting some water from Wailele Spring (near Mid-Pacific Institute; the water is said to come from the heights of Kākea). Thus a new spring, called Punahou, was created below the rocky hill, and Kauawa'ahila invited his sister in for a swim. (The first artesian well in Honolulu was drilled near Punahou, on Wilder Avenue near Metcalf Street, in 1880; water was struck at a depth of 273 feet; Fujimura and Chang 18.)

Later, Kauawa'ahila planted kalo around the spring, and "people attracted by the water and consequent fertility of the place came and settled about, voluntarily offering themselves as vassals to the twins. More and more kalo patches were excavated, and the place became a thriving settlement. The new spring, Punahou, gave its name to the surrounding area." In the meantime, the father of the twins, Kaha'akea, returned from Hawai'i Island and killed his wife Hawea for persecuting his children, then took his own life. The rocky hill is named after him. (It is also called Rocky Hill and Pu'u o Mānoa). The two rain deities returned home to Mt. Ka'ala, only "occasionally visiting Kōnāhuanui and upper Mānoa Valley, where in their rain and mist form, they may be met with today."

"Punahou" can be read in a Euromerican context as a fairy tale, with an archetypal evil stepmother, like the stepmother in Cinderella. The theme of cruelty and revenge is commonplace in such tales, and Hawea, Nakuina notes, has become "a synonym in the Hawaiian mind for a cruel stepmother."

In the context of Hawaiian culture, however, the story also describes rainfall patterns in Makiki and Mānoa and an innovation in agriculture (digging an irrigation tunnel to make relatively dry lands productive); it also establishes water rights at the new spring. Traditionally, water rights in 'auwai, or irrigation works, were divided proportionately among those who built it. The more work or workers a kalo farmer was able to provide for building and maintaining an 'auwai, the more of its water he could claim. The water at Punahou was kapu to Kauawa'ahila and Kauaki'owao and their descendants because their 'aumakua Kākea dug the tunnel that brought the water to the area. In "Ancient Hawaiian Water Rights and

Some of the Customs Pertaining to Them," Nakuina, who served as Commissioner of Private Ways and Water Rights in the district of Kona, O'ahu, describes how the konohiki of an ahupua'a also served as its luna wai, in charge of distributing water: "The konohiki of the land controlling the most water rights in a given 'auwai was invariably its luna. He controlled and gave the proportions of water to mo'o'āina, or single holdings, of the common people cultivating on that land" (80). The mo'o gods who had created the numerous underground channels connecting springs and ponds in Mānoa and Makiki, were the luna wai of the waters.

The story of the twin rain spirits does not end happily ever after, as a European fairy-tale might, with the death of the cruel stepmother. Once the land around Punahou fell into "the hands of foreigners, who did not pay homage to the twins, and who allowed the spring to be defiled by the washing of unclean articles and by the bathing of unclean persons, the twins indignantly left the place and retired to the head of Mānoa Valley." Thereafter, "the rainwater pond of Kanawai dried up." The rains Kauaki'owao and Kauawa'ahila still fall in Mānoa valley, but not as frequently over Kaha'akea as they did in previous time: "Old natives say that there is now no inducement for the gentle rain of Uaki'owao and Uawa'ahila to visit those bare hills and plains, as they would find no food there."

As in other Hawaiian narratives, there is a reciprocal relationship between the story and its setting: the story explains the relative aridity of the Punahou area today, while the aridity of the area confirms the reality of the story.

2. Pueo / Owl

"Kahalaopuna," another story by Emma M. Nakuina, tells a tradition of the pueo clan of Mānoa. (The story was published in Thrum's *Hawaiian Annual* in 1907 and is reprinted in Nakuina, *Nanaue* 33-45.) The pueo, or the native Hawaiian owl, inhabits all the islands; its favorite haunt is open grasslands, where it can be seen, both day and night, flying low over the terrain hunting for rodents. Munro wrote in 1944: "It nests in grass tufts in a hollow in the earth. The eggs are white and almost round....It was a common bird in the eighteen-nineties, but so many of its hunting grounds have been taken up for agriculture that its numbers have decreased" (67); in 1987 Pratt noted that the pueo was "uncommon" (216), with many more acres of their open hunting grounds now replaced by urban and suburban development.

The pueo was the 'aumakua of Kahalaopuna. Her grandfather was 'Aka'aka ("Laughter," or, according to Pukui's *Place Names*, "Akāka"—"Clearness"), a ridge on the east side of Mānoa; her grandmother was

Nālehua'aka'aka, "The lehua bushes of 'Aka'aka," an 'ōhi'a lehua bush growing on the ridge. Her parents were the twin deities Kahaukani ("The Hau Tree Wind"), a wind of Mānoa, and Kauakuahine ("The Sister Rain"). The marriage of brother and sister among the ali'i served to concentrate the mana of their blood in their offspring. Kahalaopuna gave off a rosy light that was a sign of her divine ancestry and mana: "Her checks were so red and her face so bright that a glow emanated from them and shone through the thatch of her house when she was inside; a rosy light seemed to envelop the house, and bright rays constantly played over the house. When she went to bathe in the spring below her house, the rays of light surrounded her like a halo. The natives maintain that this bright light is still occasionally seen at Kahaiamanō indicating that the spirit of Kahalaopuna is revisiting her old home."

Kahaiamanō, a land section in upper Mānoa, adjoining Lua'alaea ("Pit of Red Earth"), may be translated "The Shark Sacrifice": "manō" means "shark"; hai" is possibly "ha'i," a variant of "hae," which means "to tear in pieces," "to break a covenant" (Pukui-Elbert, Andrews); the place name foreshadows the tragic ending of the story.

In her youth, Kahalaopuna was betrothed to Kauhi, a young man of the manō clan from Kailua, on the other side of the Ko'olau Mountains. She became dependent on Kauhi for her poi and fish. Two men from Mānoa disfigured by makahelei ("drawn eyes") fell in love with her after hearing about her great beauty and claimed they had received love-gifts from her, even though they had never met her. Makahelei, "drawn eyes" was thought to be a punishment for breaking the kapu of one's 'aumakua: such a wrongdoer "would become humpbacked, or his eyelids would be drawn down, or he would fall lame, or suffer with chronic stomach ache or consumption—or he might be killed outright." (Kamakau, *People* 90). When Kauhi heard the rumor of Kahalaopuna's infidelity, he headed up to Mānoa from Waikīkī, filled with jealous rage and intending to kill his bride-to-be.

In the first half of the story, Kauhi takes Kahalaopuna on a westward journey toward Wai'anae, away from the protection of her grandparents and 'aumakua in Mānoa and toward the realm of the dead. (The west and the setting sun are associated in Hawaiian and Polynesian traditions with the land of the dead. One of the places on O'ahu where the spirits of the dead were said to leap into the afterworld is near the westernmost tip of the island—Ka'ena Point.) On this journey west, Kauhi killed Kahalaopuna five times: at 'Aihualama in Mānoa; at the summit of the ridge between Mānoa and Nu'uanu; at Waolani ("Heavenly Mountain Forest"), a valley on the west side of Nu'uanu; at Kilohana ("Lookout Point"), a peak near the head of Kalihi Valley; and at Pōhākea ("White Stone"), the southern pass through the Wai'anae Mountains to Lualualei, on the far west side of O'ahu. After each of her first four deaths, her 'aumakua, the pueo, restored her to life by rubbing its face against her head-bruise to heal it and breathing into her nostrils. After each resurrection, Kahalaopuna returned to Kauhi to plead her case: "'If you think I have been false to you, why not seek proof before believing it?'" Kauhi was deaf to her appeals. Finally, at Pōhākea, Kauhi buried her under the roots of a koa tree, so that her body could not be dug up by the pueo and resurrected a fifth time. Far from the valley of her grandparents and parents, Kahalaopuna's corpse was left to decay.

The pueo clan once ruled the district of Kona, O'ahu. In "Kalelealuakā and Ke'inoho'omanawanui" (Fornander, Vol. IV, 464-471), Pueonui ("Great Owl") of Kona, and Kākuhihewa, who ruled 'Ewa and adjoining districts, fought for control of O'ahu; the two eponymous heroes, after their desires for choice food and the chief's daughters were granted, helped Kākuhihewa to defeat Pueonui.

"Kapo'i" (Thrum *Hawaiian Folktales* 200-202; Kamakau *Tales* 23) records another battle in which the pueo clan defeats Kākuhihewa. The story begins by describing the origin of the clan: a man named Kapo'i lived in Kahehuna, Honolulu (upper Fort Street, near Pūowaina). He found some owl eggs one day at Kewalo ("The Calling," a land section on the east side of Pūowaina) and took them home to cook. A pueo came to beg for the life of her offspring. Kapo'i relented and the pueo became his god. The pueo told Kapo'i to build a heiau in Mānoa, and Kapo'i did so. Kākuhihewa, who was then living in Waikīkī, heard about the heiau and was offended, having declared earlier that no one could build a heiau until his own had been dedicated to the gods. Kapo'i was captured and taken to the heiau of Kūpalaha in Waikīkī, where he was sentenced to death as a rebel. A luakini heiau such as Kūpalaha required the sacrifice of a rebel for its completion (Kamakau *Works* 144). Kapo'i's god, however, summoned all the pueo of the Hawaiian Islands to rescue Kapo'i: all the pueo from Lāna'i, Maui, Moloka'i, and Hawai'i gathered in Waimānalo, at Kalapueo (the area around the Oceanic Institute at Makapu'u; the name is translated "Owl proclamation" in Pukui's *Place Names*; and "Rallying of the Owls" in Sterling and Summers); all the pueo from the Ko'olau districts of O'ahu congregated at Kanoniakapueo ("The Noni Tree of the Owl"; Pukui et al *Place Names*;) in Nu'uanu (or Kanoneakapueo, "The Dismal Cry of the Owl," around 3402 Nu'uanu Avenue; Sterling and Summers); and all the pueo from Kaua'i and Ni'ihau arrived at Pueohulunui ("Well-Feathered Owl"; Pukui et al *Place Names*;), near Moanalua Valley (a map in Ii, 96, places Pueohulunui on Waipi'o Peninsula in 'Ewa).

The distribution of these place names from one end of the Kona district of O'ahu to the other, from Makapu'u to Moanalua, suggests the great numbers of the pueo warriors. On the day of Kāne (the 27th lunar day), the pueo converged above Honolulu, darkening the sky, and a battle was fought at a place in Waikīkī that came to be called Kūkae-unahi-o-pueo ("Scaly excrement of owls") because the pueo not only scratch at the eyes and noses of Kākuhihewa's warriors, but also defecated on them. Kākuhihewa lost the battle. His warriors humbled, he acknowledged the strength of the pueo clan and allowed Kapo'i to worship his god, called Kū-kauakahi, at its heiau in Mānoa (Kamakau *Tales* 23).

In Mānoa Valley is a bluff called Pu'u Pueo, "Owl Hill," just past the fork of Mānoa Road and East Mānoa Road heading into the valley. Was this the site of Kapo'i's heiau? At Pu'u Pueo, "an avenging spirit in the form of a pueo sought to execute judgment upon a culprit for some alleged transgression, but upon the pleading of the accused for a hearing before executing punishment, it thereafter became the established custom that none should be condemned till tried and proven guilty" (Sterling and Summers 285). Just as the pueo pleaded for the lives of her offspring and Kapo'i relented, so too did the accused at Pu'u Pueo plead for a hearing and was granted one by the pueo. The pueo relented perhaps in remembrance of Kapo'i, who had listened to her pleas. This tradition of pleading for compassion and justice is connected to the story of Kahalaopuna as well: unjustly accused by Kauhi of being unfaithful, Kahalaopuna pleaded for a hearing from her accuser each time she was restored to life. Kauhi remained unrelenting in his cruelty, but in the end, a trial was held to determine the truth, and justice, if not compassion, prevailed.

A relative of Kahalaopuna, 'Elepaio (a forest bird), witnessed Kauhi's fifth murder of the princess of Mānoa at Pōhākea and reported it to her parents. Meanwhile, Kahalaopuna's spirit called to a group of passers-by for help; a young man, unnamed, but perhaps belonging to the mo'o clan, carried her body back to his home in Mō'ili'ili, where his older brother and their two spirit sisters restored Kahalaopuna to life at Mau'oki, an underground pool in Mō'ili'ili. The healing process is called "kākelekele" (cf., kākele, "to rub with oil or ointment"). The waters which restored Kahalaopuna to life were henceforth known as "The Waters of Kahalaopuna." ("Mau'oki" is also the name of a luakini heiau that was located in Mō'ili'ili at the foot of the slope separating the valleys of Mānoa and Pālolo; Sterling and Summers 279.)

The young man who saved Kahalaopuna then worked to bring her justice. He provoked Kauhi into a dispute by proclaiming that Kahalaopuna was still alive: "Kauhi then dared his rival to produce Kahalaopuna; and if the woman was not the genuine one, then his rival should be killed; on the other hand, if the woman proved to be

Kahalaopuna, then Kauhi should be declared the liar and pay for his insults with his life." A trial took place at Waikīkī, presided over by the mō'ī of O'ahu, and attended by Kahalaopuna's grandfather 'Aka'aka, who, upon Kahalaopuna's reappearance, confirmed that she was indeed his granddaughter. Kahalaopuna then told her story, and established the truth. As punishment for their wrongs against her, Kauhi, along with those of his followers who chose to die with their chief, and Kūmauna and Keawaa, the two disfigured men who provoked Kauhi's jealousy, were baked in an imu at Ulukou ("Grove of Kou Trees") on the side of the Stream of 'Āpuakēhau (an area in Waikīkī, close to where Mānoa stream used to empty into the sea; lit., "basket of dew," the name of a rain).

Kūmauna and Keawaa were transformed, through the power of their family god, into two mountain peaks in Mānoa Valley. In another version of the Kahalaopuna story, Nakuina writes: "In the eastern corner of Mānoa Valley can be seen the peak of Kūmauna, with a hump on the back of the ridge leading up to the peak, and alongside of it the ravine of Keawawa-Kiihelei. ["Awāwa" is a gulch or ravine; "Ki'ihelei" means "to straddle."] These places belonged to and are called after the two wicked men who were the cause of the sad death of Kahalaopuna" (*Hawaii: Its People, Their Legends* 45).

3. Manō / Shark

Nakuina's "Kahalaopuna," like "Punahou," does not have a happy ending. Kauhi's 'aumakua, the manō, sent a great wave over the site of the imu where Kauhi's body was burned and swept the bones of Kauhi and his followers into the sea, where they were all transformed into manō.

Like the mo'o and pueo, the manō was a helper to his descendants, often families of fishermen. The manō assisted in driving fish into nets or rescuing a fisherman whose canoe was capsized. Manō could also guide lost canoes back to land. A man named Kaiwi provided the following information about the shark 'auamkua of a fishing family named Puhi on the Big Island:

> When the Puhi go fishing, the shark appears. The 'aumakua obeys the voice of man; name the kind of fish you want and it will bring it. The men give it some of the first catch, then it disappears, and they always come back with full nets. Only when the shark appears do they have luck (hence they recognize the god's intervention). Sometimes the 'aumakua tells them beforehand in a dream that it has gathered the fish together. Besides this, the Puhi family can never be drowned. If there is a storm and the boat capsizes, the shark appears and the man rides in on its back. (Beckwith "Hawaiian Shark 'Aumakua" 504)

To rivals or enemies of the shark clan, however, the manō could be dangerous. A family of shark worshipers could send its ʻaumakua as an avenger. After a recent fatal shark attack on Maui, I heard a rumor that the woman who had been killed had tried to prevent a family of Hawaiian fishermen from crossing her property to get to their ancestral fishing ground. In the story "Nāpuaopāʻula" (Pukui, *Folktales of Hawaiʻi* 42-3), a shark family, jealous of their neighbor's beautiful daughter (their own daughter was ugly) sent its ʻaumakua to devour her. In this story, as in "Kahalaopuna," the manō is associated with jealousy. In a second version of "Kahalaopuna" (Fornander, Vol. V, 189-194), the manō and jealousy are figuratively linked in Kahalaopuna's chant to Kauhi:

> Me he manō la no ka lili iaʻu
> (Your jealousy is like a shark,)
> Ka hoʻi koke mai no nanahu iaʻu
> (Returning swiftly to bite me...)

After Kauhi's death, the pueo clan had to be on guard against the manō clan and its ocean god. ʻAkaʻaka warned his granddaughter never to go into the sea again. But one day, when the waves were breaking at Waikīkī, Kahalaopuna ignored her grandfather's warning and entered the sea to surf. In his shark form, Kauhi seized her and dragged her out to Waiʻanae, away from her family's protection once again, where he devoured her body whole, so she could not be restored to life again. Her disobedience to her kupuna led to her final demise.

The shorter version of "Kahalaopuna" in Fornander ends happily, with Kahalaopuna's restoration to life. When Kauhi came to see her again, Kahalaopuna rejected him, and thus the story ended. The fatalistic ending of Nakuina's version, with the destruction of Kahalaopuna by Kauhi, suggests a parallel to the loss of Hawaiian traditions and the overthrow of Hawaiian sovereignty by American colonizers at the end of the 19th century. In "Kaʻōpulupulu and a Prophecy," Nakuina reports the prophecy of Kaʻōpulupulu, a high priest who lived in Waimea Valley on Oʻahu's North Shore (*Hawaii Its Legends, Their Legends* 52-54). Kaʻōpulupulu heard of a plot by Kahāhana, the king of Oʻahu, to kill him, because he had protested Kahāhana's ill treatment of the people. Kaʻōpulupulu fled to Waiʻanae with his family. They were chased down and he and his eldest son were wounded by Kahāhana's warriors. As Kaʻōpulupulu laid dying, he called out to his son, "E nui ke aho a moe i ke kai, no ke kai ka hoʻi ua ʻāina"—"Take a deep breath and lay yourself down, for then the land will belong to the sea" (Pukui *ʻŌlelo* No. 363). His son then fled into the sea and died of his wounds. (Other versions say that the son was drowned at Waiʻanae, and the father was killed at Puʻuloa or at Waikīkī, where their bodies were eventually hung from coconut trees at a place of sacrifice called Helumoa, named for "the scratching of the chickens"—a place, where the maggots that fell from the bodies of the two men were eaten by chickens; or they were hung at Kūkaeunahi, a heiau, where for several weeks, their bodies did not decompose (Thrum, *Hawaiian Folktales*, 203-214; Pukui, *The Legend of Kawelo*).

Whatever the exact circumstances of the deaths of the prophet and his son, Nakuina notes: "Ka'ōpulupulu's call and advice to his son have been regarded and accepted by all Hawaiians in the nature of a prophecy, presaging the utter extinction of O'ahu's autonomy." First the island was conquered by Kahekili, king of Maui; then by Kamehameha, king of Hawai'i Island; then by haole settlers, who overthrew the monarchy in 1893 and set up a Provisional Government; finally by the United States, which annexed the islands in 1898. All of O'ahu's conquerors came by sea. Nakuina concludes: "And was this all? Or were there more scenes, as yet unenacted, when mayhap the exigencies of circumstances may cause the United States to give or abandon us to the Northern Bear, or to some great Asiatic power that may yet arise?"

This grim fatalism underlies Nakuina's three tales: "Ka'ōpulupulu and a Prophecy," "Punahou," and "Kahalaopuna." This last story can be read as a political-historical allegory. Kahalaopuna might represent the beauty of Hawaiian culture; the jealous Kauhi, who came from Kailua, outside her Kahalaopuna's home district of Mānoa and outside of her clan (her parents were siblings), can be identified with the foreigners who came in ships to take over the islands. Kahalaopuna became dependent on (and indebted to) Kauhi for food, just as Hawai'i became dependent on the American economy. Kauhi, for no just reason, jealous of the beauty of Kahalaopuna, continually beat her to death, just as the American missionaries, businessmen, and educators kept up their abusive attacks on Hawaiian culture and language after the overthrow of the monarchy and annexation. Kahalaopuna might have been saved by remaining obedient to her kupuna, just as Hawaiian culture and language might have been more strongly preserved and perpetuated by holding onto the ancestral traditions. Instead, Kahalaopuna entered the ocean against the warning of her kupuna, and was devoured by Kauhi's shark form; and Hawaiian culture was overwhelmed by Christianity and capitalism

Despite her political fatalism, Nakuina suggests at the end of her tale that Kahalaopuna and her family remain alive in their various natural-spiritual forms in Mānoa today:

> Kahaukani, the father, is known as the Mānoa wind, but his usual and visible form is the grove of hau trees, below Kahaiamanō. Kauakuahine, the mother, assumed her rain form, and is very often to be met with about the former home of her beloved child.

The grandparents also gave up their human forms and returned to Mānoa, the one to his mountain form, and the other into the lehua bushes still to be found on the very brow of the hill from which they keep watch over the old home of their petted and adored grandchild.

Kahalaopuna's story continues to speak to us through the landscape which gave it birth: a warning about the dangers of jealousy, of dependency on outsiders, and of disobedience to one's kūpuna; and a reminder of the tradition of truth and justice established by the pueo clan of Mānoa.

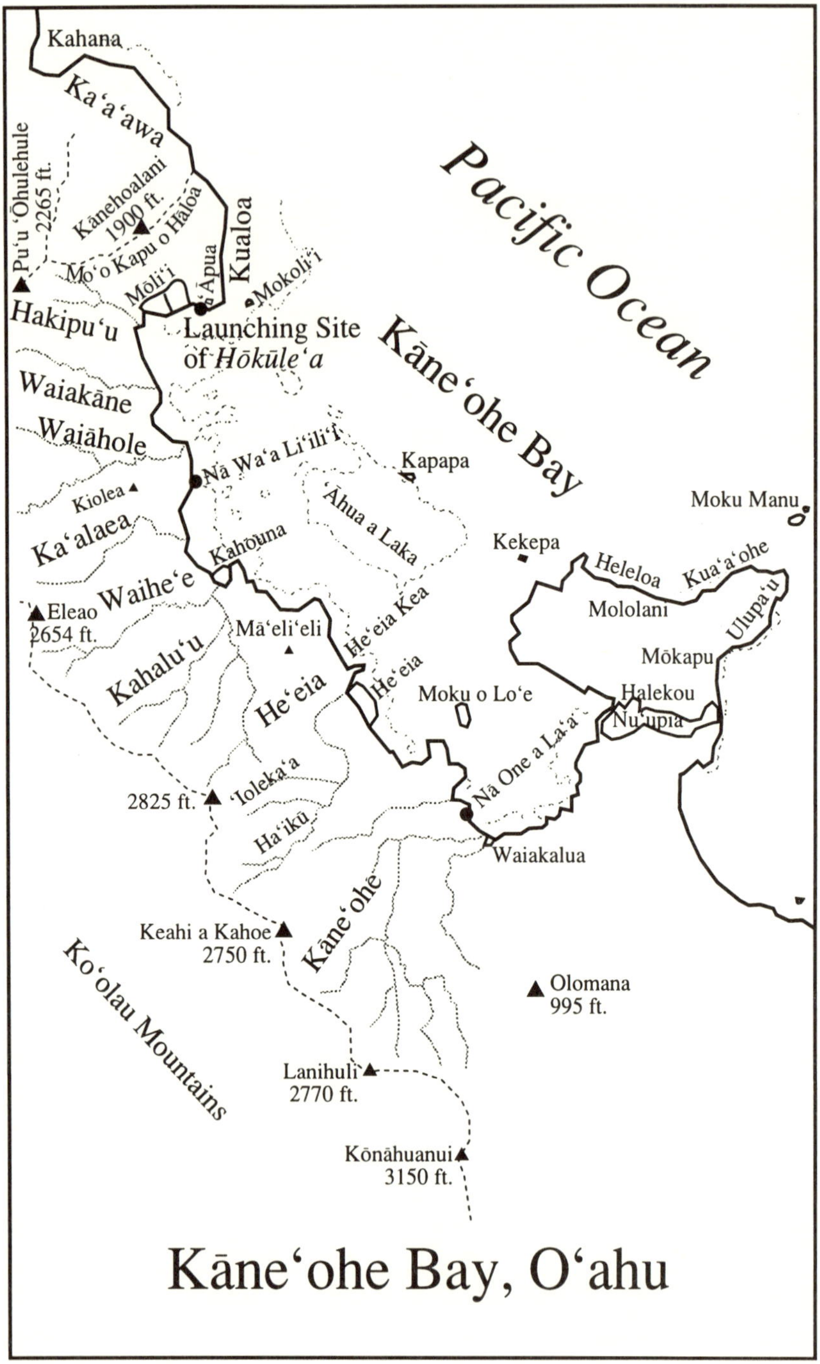
Kahana
Ka'a'awa
Pu'u 'Ōhulehule 2265 ft.
Kānehoalani 1900 ft.
Mo'o Kapu o Hāloa
Kualoa
'Āpua
Mōli'i
Mokoli'i
Hakipu'u
Launching Site of Hōkūle'a
Pacific Ocean
Kāne'ohe Bay
Waiakāne
Waiāhole
Nā Wa'a Li'ili'i
Kapapa
Kiolea
Ka'alaea
'Āhua a Laka
Moku Manu
Kahouna
Kekepa
Heleloa
Kua'a'ohe
Waihe'e
Mololani
Ulupa'u
Eleao 2654 ft.
Mā'eli'eli
He'eia Kea
Mōkapu
Kahalu'u
He'eia
Moku o Lo'e
Halekou
He'eia
Nu'upia
Nā One a La'a
2825 ft.
'Ioleka'a
Ha'ikū
Waiakalua
Kāne'ohe
Keahi a Kahoe 2750 ft.
Olomana 995 ft.
Ko'olau Mountains
Lanihuli 2770 ft.
Kōnāhuanui 3150 ft.
Kāne'ohe Bay, O'ahu

Voyaging Chiefs of Kāne'ohe Bay

Kāne'ohe Bay is surrounded by some of the most well-watered lands in Hawai'i and some of the most beautiful mountains in the world: the Ko'olau Range—peaks, two to three thousand feet high, joined by walls of sheer green cliffs. Ka Moa'e (the ENE trade winds) sweeps warm moist air into the mountains and clouds form along the summit. Rainwater has cut steep gullies into the cliffs giving them their distinctive wrinkled appearance. When it rains, dozens of thin silvery waterfalls run down the vertical gullies; half obscured by rain and mist, the waterfalls seem to pour directly from the clouds. The names of ahupua'a around the bay celebrate the life-giving water that collects in the mountains and flows through the rolling hills and flatlands into the Bay: Waiakāne ("Water of Kāne"), Waiāhole ("Water [of the] āhole fish"), Waihe'e ("Slippery water," or "Water [of the] octopus"). Water was so highly prized in ancient Hawai'i, it was synonymous with wealth and life. Such "Wai-lands" were coveted by chiefs and priests; in one version of the story of the pig-god Kamapua'a, the priest Lonoaohi, who saved Kamapua'a's life, asked for all the wai-lands of O'ahu; and the generous (or foolish) pig-god granted his wish. Kāne'ohe Bay is named for the ahupua'a and stream on its southern end: Kāne, the god of water, and 'ohe, bamboo, one of his kinolau (bodies), which flourishes on the rainy windward sides of the islands (Abbott 15; Handy and Handy 205-206).

On March 8, 1975, below the peak of Kānehoalani ("Kāne, Heavenly Companion") and the broad cliffs of Mo'o Kapu o Hāloa ("Sacred Section of Hāloa"), in Hakipu'u near the border of Kualoa at the north end of Kāne'ohe Bay, a 62-foot replica of a double-hulled voyaging canoe slid down a coconut log ramp and floated calmly at sea. The canoe was named "Hōkūle'a," "Star of Gladness," after Arcturus, the brightest star in the northern sky, and a zenith star of Hawai'i. *Hōkūle'a* had been built by the Polynesian Voyaging Society to sail an ancient migration route between Hawai'i and Tahiti, celebrated in traditional stories. This launch site was chosen because of the voyaging traditions associated with Kualoa, where the voyaging chief La'amaikahiki ("Sacred One from Tahiti") lived, and Hakipu'u, the home of a voyaging chief named Kaha'i. Other famous voyaging chiefs such as Paumakua lived in the lands around Kāne'ohe Bay. Even Laka, whose story is told throughout Polynesia, found a home in the Bay; he is said to have ruled over Ko'olaupoko, the windward district of

O'ahu (Beckwith *Hawaiian Mythology* 264), living in Waiakāne and dying either in Kualoa or at Ahua-a-Laka...

1. 'Āhua-a-Laka

On the southwestern side of the barrier reef enclosing the lagoon of Kāne'ohe Bay is a mile-long sand bar which becomes an island at low tide. When we were kids, my father would anchor there on our way back from fishing trips around the bay to let us swim and play in the shallow waters; today entrepreneurs transport tourists to the sand bar to rent them jet skis, wind-surfing boards, and snorkeling equipment. On modern maps the sand bar is labeled "Ahu o Laka," translated "Altar of Laka" (Pukui et al *Place Names*). An alternate name, 'Āhua a Laka, "Sand Bank of Laka," is suggested in a chant about Laka (Kamakau *Tales* 145-146):

> [Laka] died at Kualoa.
> To Mokoli'i, to Mokuahukele ["Island Mud Heap"],
> To the pooled sea at 'Āpua [a fishpond of Kualoa], the calm sea;
> To Makami there in Wai'āhole,
> To Hale'ula [Laka's house site] there in Waikāne,
> To Hakipu'u, to Kualoa,
> To sea, to Ahua-a-Laka ['Āhua-a-Laka],
> Laka-a-Wahieloa was taken;
> Taken by Lu'anu'u [Laka's son].
> By Lu'anu'u he was taken to the island
> To the ancestral homeland, Maui...

The chief Laka was born in Kīpahulu, Maui (or some say Hilo, Hawai'i) (Kamakau *Tales* 135-136). The chant above records his son Luanu'u's journey to transport his bones back to the sacred burial site in 'Īao, Maui, the island of Laka's birth and the home of his ancestor 'Aikanaka, of Hāna. The son of Laka and Hīkāwaolena, a chiefess of Kaua'i, Lu'anu'u grew up in his mother's homeland and came to O'ahu when his dying father summoned him (*Tales* 29).

The chant, seemingly a mere listing of stops in a journey of the spirit home, is a verbal map which may have also served as a device for remembering narratives explaining the significance of each of these places in the life of Laka. (Hawaiian chanting is an art of allusions to places.) Kamakau, in another version of the story, says Laka died at Ahua-a-Laka: "When Lu'anu'u came, he took Laka to Waikāne and shortly before his death to Ahua-a-Laka where Laka died. That place is called by his name to this day" (*Tales* 29).

Laka and Luanu'u appear 33 and 34 generations after Papa and Wākea, in the genealogy of 'Ulu, from which ruling chiefs of Hawai'i Island and

Maui trace their ancestry:

1. Wākea and Papa
......
14. Ki'i and Hinako'ula
15. 'Ulu and Kapunu'u
......
29. 'Aikanaka and Hinahānaiakamalama
30. Hema and Luamahekoa (or Ulamahehoa)
31. Kaha'i and Hinaulu'ōhi'a
32. Wahieloa and Ko'olaukahili
33. Laka and Hīkāwaelena
34. Luanu'u and Kapokulaiula

(Kamakau *Tales* 135-147; cf. Malo 238 and Kepelino 191-192. Papa and Wākea are the Earth Mother and Sky Father of Polynesian religion According to a widely accepted Hawaiian tradition, they are the first ancestors of the kanaka maoli, standing at the beginning of genealogical time. In one chant, they are said to have given birth to the islands of Hawai'i, Maui, and Kaho'olawe [Beckwith *Hawaiian Mythology* 302]. Kamakau, on the other hand, presents a genealogy in which Papa and Wākea, born at Waolani, in Nu'uanu, O'ahu, appear twenty-seven generations after the first man, Kānehulihonua ["Man made from earth"], and the first woman, Keakahulilani ["Shadow changed by heaven"]. These two "progenitors of the people of Hawai'i and of all those who dwell in the islands of the Pacific" were created by Kāne, Lono, and Kū, the main Gods of the Hawaiian pantheon at the time of European contact. The three Gods made "a model of the lands of the earth" in Kāne'ohe Bay between Kualoa and Kāne'ohe; when they saw there was no chief to rule over all things, they drew a man in the red-black soil "on the eastern flank of Mololani [a rise near Heleloa Beach on Mōkapu Peninsula], facing the sunrise and near the seashore"; then they chanted the figure to life: "Hiki au; e ola!" ["I have come; live!"] The first woman was created from the shadow of the first man [Kamakau *Tales* 130-2]. Kamakau's localized creation story contains both Polynesian and Biblical elements.)

The five descendants of 'Aikanaka and Hinahānaiakamalama down to Laka and Luanu'u are associated with voyaging. The theme of their stories is the importance of maintaining or restoring chiefly mana through contact with an ancestral homeland. Mana is the creative and procreative power of the Universe: it makes plants grow, fish and animals multiply, the human population increase; it makes human projects, such as building houses, canoes, lo'i (kalo ponds), or fishponds successful. It is embodied in "specific gods, spirits, individuals, rites, or objects. Mana was exhibited in persons, in power, strength, prestige, reputation, skill, dynamic personality, intelligence; in things in efficacy, in 'luck'; that is in accomplishment. These qualities were not mana; they were the evidences of mana, which was itself but the focussing and transmission of the potency of nature" (Handy *Polynesian Religion* 26).

A ruling chief was at the apex of Hawaiian society and had the greatest concentration of mana on earth because he was closest to the gods. His mana came from the gods from whom he was descended. He was "the means by which supernatural efficacy, mana, is conveyed to society at large. The chief is mediator, receiving and transmitting the offerings of the people to the ancestral and tribal deities. It is he who, on behalf of his people, recites the appropriate ritual formula for securing rain, bountiful harvests, success in fishing, or victory in war" (Kirch *Evolution* 37). His mana was revealed in great achievements and the wealth and productivity of his lands: "The wresting of food and material goods from nature was a fundamentally religious process precisely because the natural world was the realm of the gods. The chiefs occupied the central role in the ritual regulation of production" (38).

Because the ali'i embodied the mana of his land and people, only their lengthy genealogies were recorded in memory. Kirch points out that "descent and control went hand in hand" (257). The chiefly right to control lands was established through genealogy. Kamakau notes that "the children of the maka'āinana were taught only the names of their fathers, mothers, and grandparents" (*Tales* 80).

Chiefly genealogies record the flow of mana from the first man and woman who received the original mana from the gods, down through the generations. Narratives accompanying the genealogies tell how the ali'i maintained their mana by worship of and obedience to the gods, who required fair and just rule, and by marriage to someone of like rank; how they increased their mana through marriage with a person of higher rank; how they lost mana when they disobeyed the gods and behaved badly or committed wrongs against the people and thus, became separated from the divine source of mana.

The voyaging stories of Hawai'i record the flow of mana through ties between the new homeland (Hawai'i) and the old (Kahiki—Tahiti, or any foreign land). The voyaging canoe was the means for transporting this mana, embodied in persons or objects, from one island to another.

The story of each chief begins with his birthplace, where the mana of the gods entered him. (A form of biographical chant first composed in Hawai'i for Kapawa, 26 generations after Papa and Wākea, records the specific places where the caul, placenta, and navel cord were deposited). If the place of a chief's birth was different from the home of his maternal ancestors, the father had to return to that home to retrieve a birth-gift embodying the mana of these ancestors. (Tracing ancestry through mothers was more certain than tracing it through fathers.) The gift was something sacred, identified by the color red (ʻula). Thus, in the fifth month of his wife's pregnancy, ʻAikanaka's son Hema sailed from Hawaiʻi to the home of his wife's parents in Kahiki to get a birth-gift for his son Kahaʻi—the ʻapoʻula, a sacred wreath of red feathers, or the ʻapeʻula, possibly a sacred red kapa cloth used to wrap an image of the god Kū (Kamakau *Tales* 94). Later in this cycle of voyaging, Kahaʻi's son Wahieloa sailed from Hāna, Maui, to Punaluʻu in Kaʻū on Hawaiʻi Island, the home of his wife's maternal ancestors, to search for a birth gift called "*Alakoiula-a-Kane*" as a toy for his son Laka. (Thrum *Hawaiian Folk Tales* 112; according to Pukui-Elbert, "Ke ala koʻiʻula a Kāne" is "The rainbow-hued trail of Kāne," an allusion to death; the term in Thrum is untranslated.)

If mana was somehow held captive in a distant place, it had to be retrieved. On his voyage to Kahiki to get his son's birth-gift, Hema was captured by some fishermen, and his eyes were gouged out to be used as fish-bait (Thrum *More Hawaiian Folk Tales* 71). A chant records that Hema was "seized by the ʻāʻaia bird" (a legendary bird in the form of the ʻā, or booby; figuratively Hema "went crazy"; or the ʻāʻaia could be a symbolic reference to fishermen or a god of fishermen, as this seabird fishes in the open ocean and was a guide to finding fish.) Hema's eyes were said to be at ʻUlupaʻupaʻu, in Kahiki, where Kahaʻi went to retrieve them, treading the "ke koʻiʻula a Hema"—"the rainbow-hued trail of Hema" (Kamakau *Tales* 142). Eyes were an embodiment of mana, or more specifically knowledge, ʻike, which was based on both literal and figurative "seeing." Pukui points out that one form of ritualized cannibalism to gain mana was to scoop out and eat the eyes of an enemy (*Nānā i ke Kumu* 151).

Kahaʻi went to retrieve his father Hema's mana; at the same time he revealed his own mana through a successful voyage which is celebrated in chant (Kamakau *Tales* 142):

The rainbow was the pathway of Kahaʻi;
Kahaʻi ascended, Kahaʻi pushed on,
Kahaʻi tr[o]d the rainbow-hued trail of Hema;
The eyes of ʻAlihi [Kahaʻi's brother] gazed in bewilderment.
Kahaʻi tr[o]d along the reflected light,
The man like a canoe on the reflected light;
Above was Hānaiakamalama [the Southern Cross];
This was the pathway to seek the father of Kahaʻi,
To travel over the deep, dark ocean,
That roars at Halekumukalani.

After his search for his father's eyes, Kaha'i returned to Hawai'i and settled in Ka'ū on the island of Hawai'i, where he eventually died. (In Tahitian tradition, the mana of Tafa'i [Kaha'i] came from his mother Hinatahutahu, an underworld goddess. He descended into the underworld Pō to find his father, whose eyes had been scooped out by the gods. Tafa'i brought his blind father home and took care of him [Henry *Ancient Tahiti* 552-565]).

Kaha'i's grandson Laka sailed from Maui to Hawai'i Island to find and retrieve the bones of his father Wahieloa, who had been captured and killed by a cannibal woman named Luahine Kaikapū, his bones deposited in a cave called Kaualehu, at Kōloa, in Punalu'u, Ka'ū. (Bones, like eyes, were associated with mana; specifically, mana resided in the bones, the most durable body parts, after a person's death; bones were hidden for fear that they would be stolen by an enemy and made into fish hooks.) Laka tricked Luahine into opening the cave, then killed her, found his father's bones, and brought them back and buried them at Papa-ulu-ana, Kaumakani, in Kīpahulu, Maui. Laka's canoe was also left at this site (Beckwith 263-264).

Laka received help from his ancestors to carry out his quest—Laka's canoe was built by his divine relatives Mokuhali'i and Kupa'aike'e, gods of canoe-building; and when he went to get his father's bones he was accompanied by seven mākua ("parents," "benefactors," "providers"), including father Searcher (makua 'I'imi), who found the secret cave; father Prop (makua Poupou), who kept the mouth of the cave open, and father Stretch (makua Kiko'o) who reached into the cave and retrieved the bones (Beckwith, *Hawaiian Mythology*). These mākua personify ancestral abilities, specific kinds of mana. Apparently, after his successful quest to retrieve his father's bones, Laka moved to O'ahu, settled in Waiakāne (Photo: Landgraf 23), and left his name on the sand bar in Kāne'ohe Bay.

Variants of the stories of Hema, Kaha'i, Wahieloa, and Laka have been recorded throughout Polynesia—in Tahiti, Tuamotu, Aotearoa (New Zealand), Rarotonga, Aitutaki, and Mangaia (Cook Islands), the Marquesas, Vaitupu (Ellice Islands), Pukapuka, Sāmoa, Tonga, and the Santa Cruz Islands (Beckwith, *Hawaiian Mythology* 259-275). These stories of four generations of chiefs either originated in Hawai'i and spread elsewhere; or perhaps were brought to Hawai'i by voyaging chiefs from the South Pacific and localized by Hawaiian genealogists. In the Tahitian tradition, Kaha'i, or Tafa'i, as he is known there, was a great voyager who "fished up" (i.e. discovered) Hawai'i, a fact which is remembered in the phrase "the fish-line of Kaha'i" in a chant by Kamahualele, the foster son of Mo'ikeha, another famous voyaging chief of Hawai'i (Beckwith *Hawaiian Mythology* 355). That the story of the Hema family is so widespread in Polynesia suggests the importance of its theme: the need for the ali'i to remain connected to the mana of the homeland.

2. Kualoa-Ka'alaea-Kāne'ohe

Kāne'ohe Bay is also associated with the voyaging saga of a family of chiefs which included Mo'ikeha, his son Kila, his heir La'amaikahiki, and his grandson Kaha'i. These chiefs appear in the genealogy of Nana'ulu (Kamakau *Tales* 76-77), on which chiefs of Maui, O'ahu, Kaua'i, and Ni'ihau trace their ancestry back to Papa and Wākea.

1. Wākea and Papa
......
14. Ki'i and Hinako'ula
15. Nana'ulu and Ulukou
......
29. Maweke and Naiolaukea
30. Mulieleali'i and Wehelani
31. Mo'ikeha and Hina'aulua
32. Ho'okamali'i and Keahiula
33. Kaha'i and Kehenu

'Ulu and Nana'ulu were sons of Ki'i, who appears 13 generations after Papa and Wākea; the genealogies that flow from these two brothers run parallel to each other. Mo'ikeha's grandfather was a chief named Maweke, who appears 15 generations after Nana'ulu, making him a genealogical contemporary of 'Aikanaka, father of Hema. The sons of Maweke ruled O'ahu—Mulieleali'i in the southeastern district of Kona (Fornander *Ancient History* 48) or "the western side" of O'ahu (Kalakāua 118); Keaunui in 'Ewa; and Kalehenui in the windward district of Ko'olau (Fornander *Ancient History* 48; Kalakāua 118):

The traditions of Mo'ikeha and La'amaikahiki have been published in Fornander (Vol. IV, 112-128), Kamakau (*Tales* 77, 105-110), and Kalākaua (117-135). The broad outlines are consistent, but the details are various: Kalākaua identifies the homeland of Mo'ikeha and La'amaikahiki as Hawai'i; La'amaikahiki was a high chief of O'ahu and an adopted son of Mo'ikeha. The Fornander version says that Mo'ikeha belonged to Tahiti and that La'amaikahiki was Moi'ikeha's son by his first wife Kapo. Kamakau presents two versions. First, La'amaikahiki was a high chief of O'ahu, born to Ahukai and Keaka-milo at Kapa'ahu in Kūkaniloko, Wahiawā, the sacred birthing place of O'ahu chiefs. This chiefly child was "taken" by Mo'ikeha, perhaps in an attempt to control the future ruling chief. This taking seems to have provoked an attack by his older brother Kumuhonua, and a sea battle was fought between Kumuhonua and his younger brothers 'Olopana and Mo'ikeha. (Conflict over land and the right to rule between the senior and junior lines of a family is a common motif in Polynesian and Hawaiian chiefly traditions; Kalākaua says that 'Olopana and Mo'ikeha left O'ahu because they were not satisfied with their prospects under their older brother.) Kamakau gives a second version of the story, in which Mo'ikeha belonged to Kahiki and La'amaikahiki was a chief of Kahiki whom Mo'ikeha, after he settled in Hawai'i, designated as his heir. Whatever the case, La'a, whose name means "Sacred One," possessed great mana. The voyaging back and forth between Hawai'i and Kahiki is motivated by the need to obtain his mana.

All the stories agree that at some point Mo'ikeha, 'Olopana and his wife Lu'ukia, and La'amaikahiki were together in Tahiti or Ra'iātea, an island 120 miles WNW of Tahiti. Mo'ikeha departed for Hawai'i after some unhappy experience: either he was frustrated after a man named Mua slandered him and his lover Lu'ukia refused to sleep with him anymore (Fornander); or he was caught undoing Lu'ukia's chastity belt (a sennit lashing) for which he was "severely criticized" (Kamakau *Tales* 105); or 'Olopana was jealous of his younger brother's increasing popularity and influence, and rebuked Mo'ikeha publicly for his "extravagance and love of display" (Kalākaua 121).

Whatever his reason(s), Mo'ikeha left the southern islands and arrived at Hawai'i Island, then sailed downwind across the island chain and settled in the Puna district of Kaua'i (at Kapa'a or Wailua). He learned of a sailing contest to win the right to marry Ho'oipo, the daughter of the chief of Puna. The contest was open to "all of noble blood." Mo'ikeha chanted his genealogy from Wākea down to his grandparents Maweke and Naiolaukea and his parents Mulieleali'i and Wehelani, ruling chiefs of O'ahu (Kalākaua 128); thus, he was allowed to enter the contest and he won by beating his rivals to the island of Ka'ula 22 miles SW of Kaua'i and bringing back a palaoa (whale tooth) from the chief's representative, who had been sent there earlier. His victory was assured by La'amaomao, the god of the winds, who had come with Mo'ikeha from Ra'iātea and who carried an ipu, or gourd, from which he could call forth winds favorable to his chief. (For another story involving this Hawaiian wind deity, see M.K. Nakuina's *The Wind Gourd of La'amaomao.*)

Mo'ikeha had seven sons by Ho'oipo (Kalākaua); or three sons by Ho'oipo-i-ka-malanai, who was also known as Hina'au-lua (Kamakau); or five sons by two sisters named Ho'oipo-i-ka-malanai and Hinauu (Fornander). Three of the sons were named Ho'okamali'i, Haulani-nui-ai-ākea, and Kila, who, in all three versions, was the third and favorite son.

Mo'ikeha became the ruling chief of Puna after his father-in-law's death. As he grew old, he longed to see La'amaikahiki, the son (or foster son) he had left behind in Kahiki; or he wanted to bring his designated Tahitian heir La'amaikahiki to rule his lands in Hawai'i. Mo'ikeha held a contest to determine which of his five sons would get the honor of sailing to Tahiti to bring La'amaikahiki back (Fornander). Each of his five sons tried to send a kī-leaf canoe downstream between his thighs; only the canoe of Kila hit the mark, revealing his knowledge and understanding of the winds and currents in the stream and establishing that his mana was greater than that of his brothers. He was chosen to head the expedition south.

Kila reached Tahiti and brought La'amaikahiki back to Hawai'i (Fornander and Kalākaua); or 'Olopana refused to let La'amaikahiki go to Hawai'i, as this young ali'i was also heir to lands in Tahiti; but after 'Olopana's death, La'amaikahiki decided to sail to Hawai'i because he had heard about the fertility of the land and the industriousness of the people (Kamakau).

So sacred was La'amaikahiki, he had been hidden away in the mountains of Kapa'ahu (Fornander). Kila was required to make a human sacrifice before he could enter the marae, or temple, where La'amaikahiki was worshiping his god Lonoika'ouali'i ("Lono of the royal supremacy" or "Lono in the chiefly signs in the heavens"). La'amaikahiki brought this god to Hawai'i. Lonoika'ouali'i was the god worshiped by the Mo'o Lono (the hereditary order of Lono), one of two orders of kahuna, or priests, maintained by the 19th century king, Kamehameha I, who was the last ruling chief to worship the ancient gods: "Their rituals were those of the god Lonoika'ouali'i, the kapu lama [ritual to obtain lama trees to build fences, houses, and towers in an agricultural heiau?] and the kapu loulu [ritual for dedicating a heiau to insure peace and prosperity; loulu palm leaves were used for thatching], which were heiau rituals. Lonoika'ouali'i was the visible symbol [image] of the god Lononuiākea ["Great, broad Lono"]..." (Kamakau *People* 7; cf. Kamakau *Works* 130-144; Ii 33-45; Malo 159-176).

(The second priestly order maintained by Kamehameha I was the Mo'o Kū, the hereditary order of Kū, which carried out the rituals for the god Kūnuiākea—"Great, broad Kū," one of whose manifestations was Kūkā'ilimoku, "Ku, island snatcher," the feathered war god of Kamehameha; and the kapu 'ōhi'a kō—a ritual for cutting down 'ōhi'a trees to build structures and provide a Kū image for a heiau of human sacrifice [Kamakau *People* 7 and *Works* 130-144; Ii 33-45; Malo 159-176]. Hewahewa, the kahuna nui of the Mo'o Kū during Kamehameha's reign, was a descendant of the famous voyaging chief Pā'ao, who brought Kūkā'ilimoku to Hawai'i. Thus, the two most powerful priestly orders and gods during the time of Kamehameha I were connected with two of the most famous voyaging chiefs in Hawaiian tradition—La'amaikahiki and Pā'ao. The stories of these two chiefs were kept alive by their descendants.)

Besides introducing the god Lonoika'ouali'i to Hawai'i, La'amaikahiki also brought the pahu hula, or hula drum, and traveled about the islands teaching the art of dance accompanied by the drum (Fornander). The drum was noted for its loud voice, like the voice of a god, and hence embodying great mana. The drum brought from Tahiti by La'amaikahiki was heard in the trade winds at Hanauma Bay as La'amaikahiki's canoe crossed the Kaiwi Channel between Moloka'i and O'ahu; it was heard at Makapu'u as the canoe entered Kāne'ohe Bay (Kamakau *Tales* 109). As a receptacle of the voice of the gods, the drum was eventually used in religious ceremonies and accompanied the most sacred dances:

> ... the sounds of the pahu are referred to as leo (voice) and the drum head is referred to as waha (mouth). During state rituals in the large open-air heiau, the pahu was a receptacle for a god who spoke through the "voice" of the drum. Today, the "voices" of pahu heiau are believed still heard on certain nights of the month from the archaeological remains of heiau throughout the islands (Liner Notes, *Hawaiian Drum Dance Chants: Sound of Power in Time*).

Kalākaua emphasizes La'amaikahiki's genealogy as the source of his mana: "In his veins ran the noblest blood of Oahu. He was the son of the great grandson of the great Paumakua in direct and unchallenged descent" (133). After La'amaikahiki settled at Kualoa (Photo: Landgraf 3) on the north end of Kāne'ohe Bay, the local chiefs found three wives for him. And in a great display of procreative mana, three children were born to him, all on the same day: Lauli-a-La'a by Mano in Kāne'ohe (Landgraf 92-93); Kūkona-a-La'a by Waolena at Ka'alaea (Photo: Landgraf 35); and Ahukini-a-La'a by Hoaka-nui-kapua'i-helu at Kualoa (Kalākaua 134-135; Kamakau *Tales* 109-110).

The locations of the homes of his three wives, from the south end of Kāne'ohe Bay to the north, suggests a generous spreading of his mana over the surrounding area.

After the births of his three sons, La'a returned to Tahiti to rule over Mo'ikeha's lands there (Fornander); or to Ra'i'ātea to rule over 'Olopana's lands (Kalākaua; Kamakau does not report what happened to La'a after the triple marriage and triple birth). Fornander says that after Mo'ikeha's death, La'amaikahiki returned to Hawai'i a second time to take Mo'ikeha's bones back to the ancestral lands in Tahiti; but through his children, he left his mana in Hawai'i, becoming an ancestor to the chiefs of Hawai'i, Kaua'i, and O'ahu. "You will find his chiefly descendants in the mo'o kū'auhau (genealogy) of Nana'ulu, Puna-i-mua, and Hanala'a-nui"; Mo'ikeha's son Lauli-a-La'a, appears in Kamakau's genealogy of Nana'ulu (*Tales* 78, 110). And "From Ahukini-a-La'a Queen Kapi'olani, wife of Kalākaua, ...is recorded in descent through a line of Kauaian chiefs and kings" (Kalākaua 134-135).

At the end of Waiakalua Road, on the southern end of Kāne'ohe Bay, is a small beach park where hau trees grow along the dark brown sandy shore. On the mud flats off shore, we used to lay nets for crabs, using bloody aku heads for bait. In the late sixties, we dug for clams there, too, but the clamming was good for only two seasons; by 1969, there were too few clams, their disappearance attributed in part to "[s]oil erosion, associated with unusually heavy rain" (Devaney et al 101).

A portion of this beach is named Nā One a La'a, "The Sands of La'a."(Kamakau *Tales* 109). When La'amaikahiki's canoe arrived at Waiakalua from Hale-o-Lono, Moloka'i, a man named Ha'ikamalama chanted the mele of his drummer Kupa (which Ha'ikamalama had heard in the wind at Hanauma Bay and at Makapu'u as La'amaikahiki's canoe sailed to Kāne'ohe.) Surprised by the man's knowledge of the chant, La'amaikahiki "threw down some sand as a resting place for the canoe" and landed. The place name commemorates this landing. Ha'ikamalama was allowed to play the pahu of Kupa and made a copy of it: a gourd fitted with a shark-skin head. (Pahu were later made from hollowed-out coconut trunks or breadfruit logs as well.) Near Nā One a La'a was the house where La'amaikahiki once lived; and on a low hill nearby was his heiau, called Kalaoa (Sterling and Summers 209-210).

Just offshore of Ka'alaea, near the border of Waiāhole, is a group of small stones called "Nā Wa'a 'Li'ili'i Kiolea"—"The small canoes [of] Kiolea" (Sterling and Summers 191; Photo: Landgraf 39). Pu'u Kiolea is the highest peak on the ridge that runs from the Ko'olau mountains down toward the stones. Kiolea is "a high, unsafe seat," perhaps a local lookout (or Kī-o-Lea, "the ti plant of Lea"?; cf. "Ka-ipu-o-Lea" in the chant below). The offshore rocks are said to be the remains of canoes that brought sands and "a mapu tree" from Tahiti. The sands nearby are called the sands of La'amaikahiki—a safe landing place for canoes (Photo: Landgraf 37):

I Onehuna, i Onehali
(At Hidden-sands, at Fetched-sands)
A kele 'akiu, a kelekele 'akiu,
(Sail to safety, sail, sail to safety)
Ke one i Māhinahina,
(At the sands of Māhinahina)
Ka-ipu-o-Lea lā.
(Is the gourd of Lea).

Onehuna—the sands hidden (hūnā) perhaps because the landing place was submerged at high tide; or because it was known only to local residents. Or Onehuna could mean "fine, powdery (huna) sand."

"Fetched-sands" recalls the tradition of La'amaikahiki throwing down sand at Waiakalua—a practice perhaps established by him to create canoe landing sites around the Bay. Lea ("the gourd of Lea") is a goddess of canoe-building, suggesting this place was not just a site for landing, but for building and launching canoes:

Ē Mokuhāli'i, Kūpā'aike'e, Lea,
(O Mokuhāli'i, Kūpā'aike'e, Lea,)
Eia ka pua'a
(Here is the pig,)
He uku, he makana, he 'ālana
(A reward, a gift, an offering,)
He mōhai iā 'oukou
(A sacrifice to you.)
Ua pa'a ka wa'a [inoa]
(The canoe [name] is finished,)
A e ho'olana 'ia aku ana i ke kai...
(Ready to be launched in the sea)

(Pukui "Canoe Making" 25; cf. Gutmanis 79)

A kapu haunts the stones of "Nā Wa'a Li'ili'i": once a haole road-builder came to take the stones. He ordered his men to break up the stones and carry the pieces off. The native workers refused; the haole workers complied. The haole road-builder and workers all died soon after their desecration of the site.

On the north end of Kāne'ohe Bay the ahupua'a of Kualoa ("Long Back") lies beneath the peak of Kānehoalani (Photo: Landgraf 7). The cliffs of Palikū fall away to either side; the cliffs are also called Mo'o Kapu o Hāloa ("Sacred Section of Hāloa"). Hāloa was the son of Wākea by his daughter Ho'ohōkūkalani. Born a shapeless mass, Hāloa was buried in the ground and reborn as kalo, the Hawaiian staff of life. Hāloa means "Long Breath" or "Long Life." Hā, or breath, like the eyes and the bones, is associated with mana. It could "impart mana, 'magical power,' as when a priest would exclaim 'Hā!' (Pukui and Korn *The Echo of Our Song* 26). The breath of a god could bring or restore a person to life.

After the first Hāloa became the kalo plant, another son was born in human form, and was also called Hāloa, an ancestor of La'amaikahiki (Kamakau *Tales* 134). While he was in Hawai'i, this famous voyaging chief lived beneath these sacred cliffs, named for one of his ancestors.

3. Hakipu'u

Mo'ikeha's grandson Kaha'i-a-Ho'okamali'i (Ho'okamali'i was Mo'ikeha's first son) was also a voyager, famous for having sailed to

Wawau, ʻŪpolu, and Savaiʻi (Possibly places in Sāmoa and Tonga, but more likely in Tahiti Nui—Wawau, ʻŪpolu, and Savaiʻi, or Havaiʻi, were ancient names for Borabora, Tahaʻa, and Raʻiātea.) Kahaʻi-a-Hoʻokamaliʻi brought back a breadfruit tree from ʻŪpolu and planted it in Puʻuloa, ʻEwa, where his father lived (Kamakau *Tales* 108). Another tradition says that Kahaʻi lived in Hakipuʻu (Photo: Landgraf 15), next to Kualoa, and it was there he planted a breadfruit tree he brought back from ʻŪpolu (Sterling and Summers 186). The breadfruit tree embodies mana in food plant form, a blessing to the people. (In one tradition, the god Kū is said to have turned upside down and become a breadfruit tree in order to feed his family during a famine; see Pukui *Folktales* 8). For the gift of this food plant, Kahaʻi is remembered. Because of his daring voyages, Kahaʻi was honored by the aliʻi: "He was raised by the chiefs to their own kingly rank. And never again need he lower his sail—not for a chief nor a priest nor a king.... It is said that in 1795, when the conquering chief [Kamehameha] rounded this island [Oʻahu], [he] lowered his sail [when he passed Hakipuʻu] to show his respect for the daring Kahaʻi." (Sterling and Summers 186). (Was this Kahaʻi the same Kahaʻi as Moʻikeha's son, or a namesake? Moʻikeha's son was already a chief and would not have had to be "raised by the chiefs to their own kingly rank.")

Another tradition asserts that the lowering of sails in north Kāneʻohe Bay was out of respect for the sacredness of Kualoa, which was a training ground of chiefs as well as a puʻuhonua, a place of refuge where those condemned to death could seek safety (Sterling and Summers 178).

4. Mōkapu

In the ʻUlu genealogy, ten generations after Hema, is a voyaging chief named Paumakua, who was born at Kua-ʻa-ʻohe (Kua-wa-ʻohe), between the land sections of Heleloa and Ulupaʻu Crater, on Mōkapu Peninsula (Photos: Landgraf 71, 77, 79), which embraces the southern end of Kāneʻohe Bay. (This Paumakua was perhaps a namesake of the one whom Fornander identifies as the great grandfather of Laʻamaikahiki.) In the time of Auanini, the grandfather of Paumakua, the first haole arrived off of Mōkapu in a ship named *Ulupana*. Molo Lana was the ship's captain; Malaea, his wife; and Olomana, Aniani, and Holokamakani, crew members. The story implies that the famous peak below Kōnāhuanui in Kailua was named after this Olomana (Kamakau *Tales* 113; a different tradition of the naming of Mt. Olomana is given in Pukui's *Place Names*). Paumakua went voyaging to foreign lands, perhaps to the lands of these haole visitors. A chant (Kamakau *Tales* 96) celebrates his voyaging achievements:

Paumakua, the chief of Moena-i-mua,

The chief who traveled to Kahiki,
To Kahiki in the wide sea,
The gentle, the precious, the swift-moving one.

Paumakua is said to have brought back white kāhuna (priests, or experts in some art or profession) named Ka'eka'e and Maliu, and a white ka'ula (prophet) named Malela. Malela's eyes are remembered for expressing his great mana: Ka haole nui maka 'ālohilohi; he āholehole maka 'a'ā; ka pua'a ke ke'oke'o nui maka 'ula'ula": "The big foreigner with bright sparking eyes, a young āhole fish with staring eyes; the large white pig with reddish eyes" (Kamakau *Tales* 95-97). The story of Paumakua shows that the chiefs of Hawai'i were not afraid to bring mana (knowledge, expertise, power of prophecy) from a foreign source through voyaging to support the mana of a chief in Hawai'i. Many generations later, Kamehameha enlisted haole who were experts in Western weaponry to defeat his rivals.

5. The Modern Revival of Voyaging

By the time Captain Cook reached the Hawaiian Islands in 1776, voyages between Hawai'i and Tahiti and other foreign land were distant memories of the traditional past. The last voyage to and from the South Pacific recorded by the genealogical chants of Hawai'i was made by the priest Pā'ao, five generations after Paumakua, in the time of La'au. Pā'ao came to Hawai'i from Wawau (Borabora) and Taha'a ('Ūpolu) (Kamakau *Tales* 97), after a dispute with his brother Lonopele. When he arrived, Lanakawai (or Lonokawai) was the ruling chief of Hawai'i Island. Pā'ao lived on Hawai'i "until the kings of Hawaii became degraded and corrupted (hewa)" (Malo 6); they had "sinned by intermarriage with commoners, thus diluting the sacred blood" (Pukui *Folktales* 69). Like Mo'ikeha's son Kila, Pā'ao sailed to Tahiti to bring back a chief who would replenish the mana in Hawai'i from its source in the South Pacific. Pā'ao brought back with him Pilika'aiea to replace La'au, the chief who ruled after Lanakawai: "... Pili ruled as mō'ī after La'au. You will see Pili there in the line of succession, the mo'o kū'auhau [genealogy] of Hanala'a-nui [a branch of the 'Ulu genealogy]" (Kamakau *Tales* 100). The chiefs of Hawai'i Island down to Kamehameha trace their ancestry from Pili; the priests of Kū under the ruling chiefs were descendants of Pā'ao (Pukui, *Folktales* 69).

Why did voyaging end after Pā'ao? The motive of voyaging was to maintain contact with a distant homeland, the original source of mana. After the ruling chiefs had obtained the mana of Pili, they maintained it through intermarriage among their own ranks (Kame'eleihiwa *Native Land*, 40-44), righteous government and behavior, proper worship of the gods, and innovations which made the land prosperous. Thus, there was no longer a need for ties with the ancestral homeland. After Pili's arrival in Hawai'i, archaeological evidence indicates a period of remarkable expansion of the productive capabilities of Hawaiian agriculture, aquaculture (the fishponds associated with Kū'ula kai), and fishing. The population grew into the hundreds of thousands.

The ruling chiefs had the mana to sustain their communities in productive and healthy isolation for six centuries after Pā'ao—without metal, fossil fuels, electricity, engines, electronics, manufactured chemicals, plastics, and other modern inventions. Menzies, a naturalist with the British explorer Vancouver, described Waikīkī in 1792:

> ...The verge of the shore was planted with a large grove of cocoanut palms, affording a delightful shade to the scattered habitations of the natives...We pursued a pleasing path back into the plantation, which was nearly level and very extensive, and laid out with great neatness into little fields planted with taro, yams, sweet potatoes, and the cloth plant [wauke] (qtd. in Handy and Handy 482).

With the coming of foreigners, the mana of the ruling chiefs and people was severely tested. The kanaka maoli suffered the loss of family members to introduced diseases, such as small pox, tuberculosis, influenza, and measles, their population plummeting from an estimated 800,000 to 40,000 during the 19th century (Stannard 50-52); the loss of their gods, when the ruling chiefs abandoned their native religion and became Christian converts (1819); the loss to foreign capitalists of lands once held by the chiefs for the common good and made sacred by the gods; the loss of sovereignty, when a group of haole businessmen, with the support of U.S. Marines, overthrew the Hawaiian monarchy and took control of government and education (1893). Hawaiian children were forbidden to speak their native language in English-only schools. In the 19th and 20th centuries, an influx of immigrants, brought from Asia and other parts of the world by capitalists to create a pool of inexpensive labor, further weakened the Hawaiian language and culture. Today, the islands are multiethnic, with those of Hawaiian ancestry making up less than 20% of the population.

In this context of almost two centuries of assault on the mana of the kanaka maoli, the voyaging canoe *Hōkūle'a* was launched at Kualoa in 1975. What was originally planned as an scientific experiment to test a theory of Polynesian migration became part of a revival that included not just voyaging, but language, ceremony and protocol, hula and chant, canoe-building, kalo farming, kapa-making, featherwork, wood-carving, lua (a martial art), and so on. People practicing these traditional arts have begun to re-establish a healthy relationship between themselves and the land and sea and to reveal the mana inherent in the successful performance of these arts.

Hōkūle'a's first voyage from Hawai'i to Tahiti took place in 1976, and despite conflict between two factions on the canoe, the voyage was a success. Those who thought that the oral traditions recounting such voyages were fictions and who doubted that traditional navigational techniques could be used to guide sailing canoes across 2,400 miles of open ocean were proven wrong (Finney *Hōkūle'a*). The navigator of *Hōkūle'a* was Mau Piailug from Satawal, a tiny atoll in the Caroline Islands of Micronesia, where the ancient traditions of navigating by celestial bodies, winds, ocean swells, and sealife had survived into the 20th century (Lewis). An aging Tevake, the last known Polynesian navigator, from Pileni Atoll in the Santa Cruz Reef Islands, had left in his canoe in 1970 and disappeared at sea. According to one source: "Tevake made something in the nature of a formal farewell before his departure from Nufilole, and it would seem that either he had a premonition of disaster or, more likely, that he simply paddled out to sea in the manner of the Tikopians and did not intend to arrive" (Lewis 309). He had chosen a navigator's death.

In 1980, *Hōkūle'a* made a second voyage to Tahiti, this time navigated by Nainoa Thompson, a descendant of ali'i from Hawai'i Island on his mother's side and from Kaua'i and Maui on his father's side. He had studied traditional navigation with Mau, but also Western astronomy, oceanography, and meteorology to speed up the learning of traditional techniques. (Mau was trained as a navigator from infancy, when he was placed in tide pools so he could feel the movements of the ocean; Nainoa began his study as a young man in his 20's.) After guiding *Hōkūle'a* 4,800 miles to Tahiti and back, Nainoa sighted the island of Hawai'i (Kyselka *Ocean in Mind*), just as Mo'ikeha, La'amaikahiki, and Pā'ao had done centuries earlier.

The 1976 and 1980 voyages of *Hōkūle'a* rekindled an interest among the kanaka maoli in reconnecting with ancestral homelands to the South. Other voyages followed—to Aotearoa (New Zealand) in 1985-1987; to Rarotonga in the Cook Islands in 1992; to Nukuhiva in the Marquesas Islands in 1995. Each voyage has been a reenactment of the past, as well as a rite of passage for young kanaka maoli seeking mana from ancestral spirits and wisdom in traditional ways.

In 1929, on a Bishop Museum expedition, anthropologist Te Rangi Hiroa (Peter Buck) visited the marae of Taputapuātea in the district of Opoa, on the island of Ra'iātea. The marae was once the most sacred place in all of Polynesia—the center of the Polynesian world, the head of the octopus of Ta'aroa (Kanaloa), a place where canoes were built and navigation was taught. In the wake of colonialism and the Pacific-wide suppression of Polynesian culture and religion, the marae was in ruins.

Standing there, the half-Maori, half-Irish Buck lamented the loss of Polynesian mana:

> I had made my pilgrimage to Taputapu-atea, but the dead could not speak to me. It was sad to the verge of tears. I felt a profound regret, a regret for—I know not what. Was it for the beating of the temple drum or the shouting of the populace as the king was raised on high? Was it for the human sacrifices of olden times? It was for none of these individually but for something at the back of them all, some living spirit and divine courage that existed in ancient times and of which Taputapu-atea was a mute symbol. It was something that we Polynesians have lost and cannot find, something that we yearn for and cannot recreate. The background in which that spirit was engendered has changed beyond recovery. The bleak wind of oblivion had swept over Opoa. (Buck 85)

Sixty-three years after Te Rangi Hiroa's visit, in 1992, *Hōkūle'a* stopped at Taputapuātea on its way to Rarotonga to participate in a festival of Pacific arts, which was celebrating the revival of Polynesian and Pacific voyaging inspired by the canoe's travels. After entering Te Ava Moa ("The Sacred Pass") and anchoring in the lagoon off Taputapuātea, the crew, some of whom traced their ancestry back to Ra'iātea, were welcomed onto the marae. The gift the crew brought with them was a pahu drum named Poki'i ("Younger sibling"), carved from a coconut log, with a shark-skin head lashed on; it was a descendant of the first pahu brought to Hawai'i from Tahiti by La'amaikahiki centuries earlier.

At Opoa, a gathering of Polynesian navigators took place, organized by Nainoa Thompson. New navigators from Hawai'i, the Cook Islands, and Aotearoa discussed their sail plans and course strategies for voyages they were about to make, or had just made. The meeting at Opoa was attended by Mau Piailug, who had made this revival of Polynesian wayfinding possible through the sharing of his knowledge with Hawaiians eager to learn. The gathering was a way of showing Mau (an honorific name meaning "Brave") that his knowledge of wayfinding was being passed on to others; once planted by his teaching, it had rooted, branched, leafed, flowered, and was now bearing fruit. Through the recovery of traditional knowledge and beliefs, the mana that Te Rangi Hiroa lamented had been lost forever to "the bleak wind" of colonialism was re-emerging at the end of the 20th century.

Since 1975, *Hōkūle'a* had traveled far from its place of birth in Kāne'ohe Bay; its successes have shown that its birth was an auspicious one, that the canoe was pleasing to the gods (Polynesian Voyaging Society WWW Site. http://leahi.kcc.hawaii. edu/org/pvs).

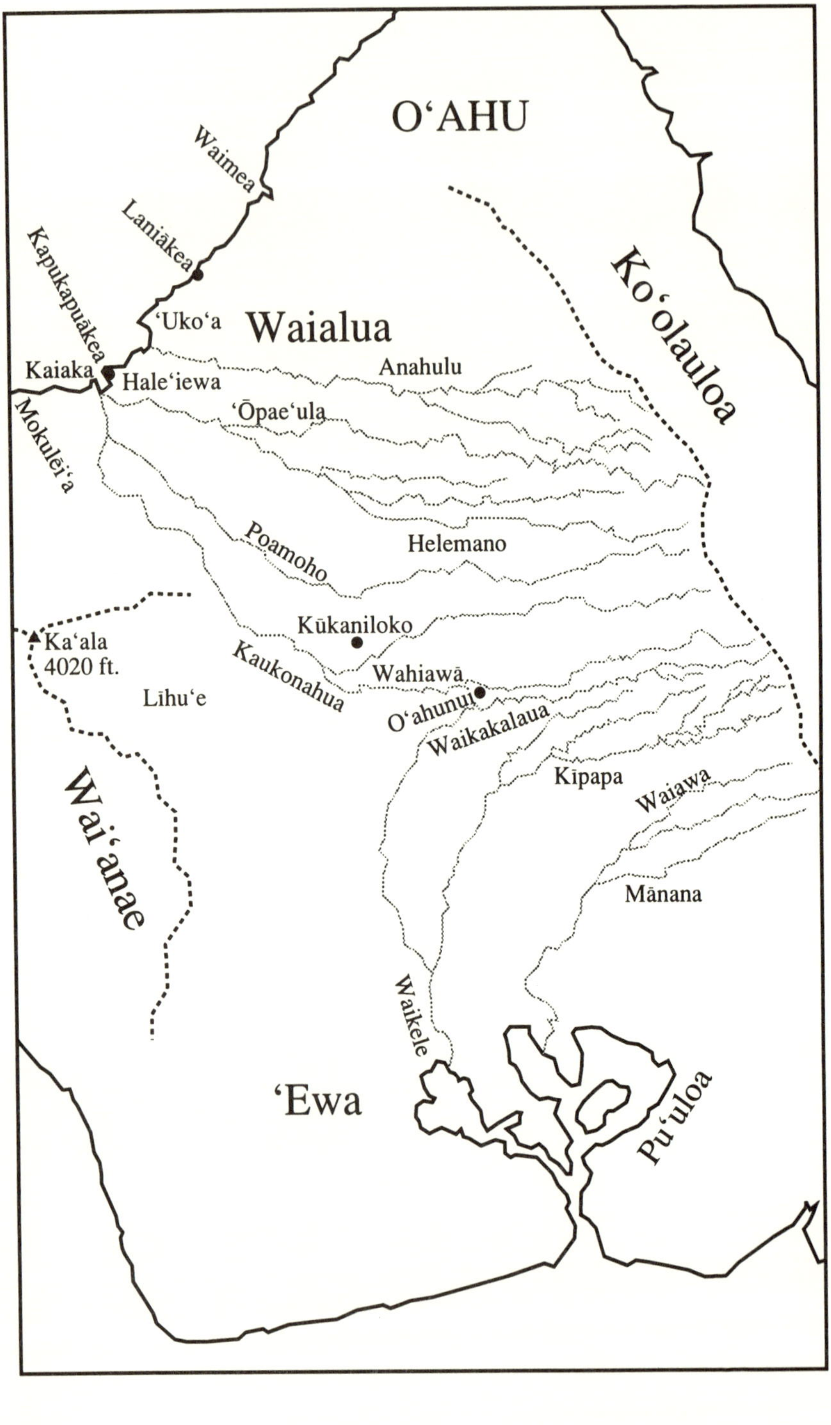
O‘AHU
Waimea
Laniākea
Kapukapuākea
‘Uko‘a
Waialua
Ko‘olauloa
Kaiaka
Hale‘iewa
Anahulu
Mokulēi‘a
‘Ōpae‘ula
Poamoho
Helemano
Kūkaniloko
Ka‘ala
4020 ft.
Kaukonahua
Wahiawā
Līhu‘e
O‘ahunui
Waikakalaua
Kīpapa
Waiawa
Wai‘anae
Mānana
Waikele
‘Ewa
Pu‘uloa

Killing the Cannibal King

1. Birthing Stones & Cannibal Stones

Atop the gently rising plateau between the Koʻolau and Waiʻanae Mountains, near the town of Wahiawā, is the geographical center of Oʻahu. Four streams—Opaeʻula, Helemano, Poamoho, and Kaukonahua—emerge from valleys in the Koʻolau Mountains and flow north, cutting gulches across the plateau before emptying into Kaiaka Bay in the district of Waialua. Streams whose headwaters are south of Kaukonahua—Waikakalaua, Kīpapa, Waiawa, Mānana—flow south, into the estuary of Puʻuloa in ʻEwa.

Just off the highway between Wahiawā and Whitmore Village, surrounded by a grove of eucalyptus trees in the middle of pineapple fields, is the royal birthing stone of Kūkaniloko. The stone was established by the aliʻi Nanakaōko and his wife Kahihiokalani for the birth of their son Kapawa. (Nanakaōko, who lived in Wahiawā and Līhuʻe in Waialua, appears on the ʻUlu genealogy 24 generations after Papa and Wākea.) The site of the stones is described by Kamakau:

> A line of stones was set up on the right hand and another on the left hand, facing north. There sat thirty-six chiefs [eighteen on each side]. There was a backrest, a kuapuʻu, on the upper side; this was the rock Kūkaniloko, which was the rock to lean against. If a chiefess entered and leaned against Kūkaniloko and rested on the support to hold up the thighs in observance of the Līloe kapu [the prescribed regulations for birthing], the child born in the presence of the chiefs was called an aliʻi, an akua, a wela—a chief, a god, a blaze of heat. (*Tales* 38)

After the royal birth, the newborn infant was taken about 300 yards south to a heiau called Hoʻolonopahu ("Listen to the pahu drum"), where forty-eight chiefs attended the cutting of the navel cord. Four hundred yards west was the location of the sacred drum called Hāwea, which sounded to announce the chief's birth. Commoners and kauwā (a class of outcasts) attended at a farther distance, to the east and south (Kamakau *Tales* 38).

"Oʻahunui" by Emma M. Nakuina (published in Thrum's *Hawaiian Annual* in 1897, reprinted in *Ancient Oʻahu* 51-57) opens with a reference to Kūkaniloko, "the ancient birthplace of the O'ahu kings and rulers" and the headquarters of the "high priest of the island": "Every woman of royal blood had to retire to this place when about to give birth to a child, on pain of forfeiting the rank, privileges, and prerogatives of her expected offspring, should the child be born in a less sacred place."

O'ahunui, located a few miles east of Kūkaniloko, was the former residence of the ruling chiefs of O'ahu. A stone in the shape of the island of O'ahu is said to rest there (Sterling and Summers 137). According to Nakuina's story, the last ali'i to live at O'ahunui was named O'ahunui. (No ali'i by this name appears in the genealogies of Malo, Kamakau, or Kepelino.) O'ahunui took to eating human flesh under the influence of cannibal chiefs called Lō-'Aikanaka, who came from the South Seas and settled at Mokulē'ia in Waialua. "'Aikanaka" means, literally, "people-eater," metaphorically, a strong warrior or a ruler of men (A chief named 'Aikanaka appears in the 'Ulu genealogy as the father of Hema; he resided in Hāna, Maui, and was known as an industrious and kind chief, not a cannibal [Beckwith *Hawaiian Mythology* 241-243]; according to one Tahitian tradition, Nona, the grandmother of Hema, was a cannibal [Henry *Ancient Tahiti* 552]).

Kamakau identifies Lō-ali'i as high-ranking chiefs, who belonged to Līhu'e, Wahiawā, and Halemano [Helemano]—[places in central O'ahu (*Tales* 40; *People* 5). According to Kepelino, the Lō-ali'i were "called lō, because they kept up their kapu as chiefs even though they did not live with the ruling chiefs of the island but dwelt apart in the mountains" (196). The term "lō," according to Kamakau, is from "loa'a," "to obtain"; these chiefs guarded their kapu by living apart and thus from their ranks, "a 'guaranteed' chief might be obtained. ...They were like gods, unseen, resembling men." (*Tales* 40). How, or whether, these lō-ali'i were connected to the Lō-'Aikanaka of Nakuina's "O'ahunui" is not clear; however, both are said to have lived in the mountains (i kuahiwi) of central O'ahu.

According to "O'ahunui," the Lō-'Aikanaka were driven from Mokulē'ia inland by the residents of Waialua "exasperated by the frequent demands on them to furnish bodies for the cannibal feasts." The cannibal chiefs fled upland and settled at Helemano, eight miles east of Hale'iwa in Pa'ala'a (McAllister 137), mauka of Kūkaniloko, toward Waimea. From Helemano, these cannibal chiefs continued to send their warriors on forays to capture victims for their feasts. They invited O'ahunui to one of their feasts and fed him human flesh; the king found it to his liking, developed an irresistible craving for it, and took every opportunity to dine with his new friends. One day he sent his brother-in-law Lehuanui, a priest, to 'Uko'a fishpond in Waialua for some āholehole (an 'ono fish, brought to Waialua by the goddess Ihukoko). In Lehuanui's absence, O'ahunui killed his two plump nephews, potential rivals to his rule, and had them cooked and served to him. The spirits of the two children appeared to their father and told him of their uncle's abomination. Lehuanui rushed home and discovered that his sons had indeed been consumed. Their skulls were hanging from an ʻōhiʻa lehua tree, their bones buried beneath. Enraged, Lehuanui entered the Oʻahunui's sleeping house and beheaded him as he slept "satiated on an excess of human flesh and copious cups of ʻawa....The headless body of Oʻahunui lay where he was killed, abandoned by everyone. In time, it ...turned to stone as a witness to the anger of the gods and their detestation of his horrible crime." Lehuanui also killed his wife, Kilikiliʻula, for not protecting their children. She too turned to stone, as did all the servants who had participated in the cannibalism. The god Kāne cursed the spot, and "no one has lived there since."

The story of Oʻahunui begins with what was most sacred and ends with what was most heinous in Hawaiian tradition. The Kūkaniloko birthing stone symbolizes the most exalted event—a royal birth. The highest value was placed on life and the most valuable life was that of a ruling chief, who embodied the mana of his divine ancestors, which had to be protected and maintained through pono (just) behavior for the health and productivity of his land and people. The cannibal stones located a few miles away from the birthing stones stood as a reminder of the most horrific crime—consuming the life of children, in this case his nephews, taking from the future to satisfy the perverse cravings of the present. Because his act desecrated the area, the royal residence at Oʻahunui was abandoned and eventually moved to Waikīkī. Kamakau places this move during the time of the mōʻī (king) Māʻili-kūkahi: "Soon after he became mōʻī, the chiefs took Māʻili-kūkahi to Waikīkī to live; he was perhaps the first of the ruling chiefs to live there. Until then the chiefs had lived in Waiʻalua and ʻEwa" (54).

Beckwith notes that "there is no proof that cannibalism was ever practised in the Hawaiian group" (340). But before it was planted over by pineapple fields (McAllister 140), the site at Helemano where the Lō-ʻAikanaka supposedly held their cannibal feasts attracted 19th century tourists. The story of the cannibal king of central Oʻahu became popular in travel accounts: Gilbert Farquahar Mathison (*Narrative of a Visit to Brazil, Chili, Peru, and the Sandwich Islands... During the Year 1821-1822*) described to his readers the cannibal king's stone platter, on which the king supposedly carved up his victims. James J. Jarves (*Scenes and Scenery in the Sandwich Islands During 1837-1842*) described the site of the cannibalism: "The ruins of an extensive heiau can still be traced, and the site of the house of the chief, who was the terror of the island. Near it, is a large flat stone, which goes by the name of ipu kai, or meat platter."

C.R. Whittemore ("Trip around the island of Oahu...Mar. 16, 1895") reported "Our hosts showed us a rock where in olden times, they slaughtered, roasted and ate human beings. Tradition is that it was over two hundred years since that had happened and only rulers could do it then." (See Sterling and Summers 107-112.)

These 19th century reports of Hawaiian cannibalism are part of a Pacific-wide myth, spread by European and American writers. Robert Louis Stevenson (*In the South Seas: The Marquesas, Paumotus and Gilbert Island*, 1900) declared "'Cannibalism is traced from end to end of the Pacific, from the Marquesas to New Guinea, from New Zealand to Hawaii....All Melanesia appears tainted....'" (qtd. in Sacks 215).

The most widely read account of Polynesian cannibalism was Herman Melville's *Typee: A Peep at Polynesian Life During a Four Months' Residence in A Valley of the Marquesas* (1846). Melville claimed that his book represented the "unvarnished truth," although scholars point out that Melville was on the island of Nukuhiva for about one month, not four months as his subtitle claims; and some of the things which he says he witnessed were borrowed from accounts of earlier travelers (Melville 313). The lake he describes sailing on with a Marquesan girl is also fictitious. The plot of *Typee* builds to a climax that hinges on whether or not the narrator, Tommo, is going to escape or be consumed by his allegedly cannibalistic captors, a tribe called Typee (spelled "Taipi" in modern anthropological texts). The narrator never actually witnesses cannibalism, but he claims to have seen in "a curiously carved vessel of wood" "the disordered members of a human skeleton, the bones still fresh with moisture, and with particles of flesh clinging to them here and there!" (265); he concludes that the Taipi had eaten three recently slain enemy warriors. The assertion that a story is the "unvarnished truth" is, of course, merely a convention of travel writing, and Melville (as opposed to his narrator) seems to suspect that the cannibalism may be an illusion: he apparently confessed to his wife that "he never had evidence that it was a custom of the tribe"; but as Paul Lyons points out, "However much his book parodies fears of cannibalism, Tommo/Melville remains haunted and obsessed by the subject" (Lyons 40-42), and his credulous Christian audience, hungry for stories about the savagery of non-Christians, swallowed the book as if it were fact.

The European and Euroamerican desire to believe in the cannibalism of natives in the Pacific and elsewhere, often without any direct or corroborating evidence of it, was self-serving. (See Arens, *The Man-Eating Myth*; Lyons 38-39.) As Europeans began leaving their shores in the 15th century to search for resources to feed the growing capitalist system and later, to establish markets to consume its products, they encountered indigenous peoples in practically every piece of inhabitable land on earth, including the most remote islands of the Pacific. "Cannibalism" became emblematic of "Savagery," a justification for conquering, converting, enslaving, or killing the natives they encountered, while appropriating their resources and lands. European scholars argued over an either/or fallacy: were the indigenous peoples innately perverse and therefore, unredeemable, or were they Noble Savages who could be saved? (Arens 78). The assumption that the indigenous peoples were at a lower stage of biological, cultural, or ethical development was not often questioned. But Arens has argued that the belief that Christians had the moral right to conquer and rule because the natives were cannibals was invalid because its premise was unsupported—there has never been reliable eyewitness account of native cannibalism (181). Whether there was evidence of cannibalism or not, it was absurd to argue that European colonizers were more "civilized" than natives. As the 17th century French scholar Montaigne points out in his essay "Of Cannibals," Christians perpetrated acts even more inhumane than cannibalism in the name of their God—they tortured their victims alive:

> I think there is more barbarity in eating a man alive than in eating him dead; in tearing by tortures and the rack of body still full of feeling, in roasting a man bit by bit, in having him bitten and mangled by dogs and swines (as we have not only read but seen within fresh memory, not among ancient enemies, but among neighbors and fellow citizens, and what is worse, on the pretext of piety and religion) than in roasting and eating him after he is dead. (155)

Natives sometimes repeat stories of cannibalism jokingly, serving up to gullible visitors what they think these visitors might want to ingest (Lyons 34). Tanaoa, a native of Tahuata I met in the Marquesas Islands, took great delight in pretending to gnaw on a human forearm or a freshly caught fish to "confirm" the Euroamerican belief in Marquesan "savagery." The joke is on ignorant tourists and travelers who crisscross the globe in order to validate the prejudices they lug around with them like so much baggage.

Melville reports the curious case of an old chief who claimed to have eaten the big toe of Captain Cook: "His indignant countrymen actually caused him to be prosecuted in the native courts, on a charge nearly equivalent to what we term defamation of character; but the old fellow persisting in his assertion, and no invalidating proof being adduced, the plaintiffs were cast in the suit, and the cannibal reputation of the defendant fully established. This result was the making of his fortune; ever afterwards he was in the habit of giving very profitable audiences to all curious travelers who were desirous of beholding the man who had eaten the great navigator's big toe" (*Typee* 261). Ironically, while Melville jokes about this old chief's sly subterfuge to gain notoriety and make money, he himself used a similar trick, profiting greatly from the sales of *Typee,* which became a best-seller partly because it contained an allegation of cannibalism. Melville became known as "the man who lived among cannibals."

More recently, travel writer Paul Theroux, wanting to sell a book entitled *The Happy Isles of Oceania* and feeling compelled to say something outlandish about Pacific Islanders, jokingly invented a new myth of cannibalism. No longer able to claim, like Melville, that he had lived among Pacific Island people-eaters, he speculates that "the people-eaters of the Pacific had all evolved, or perhaps degenerated, into Spam eaters" because "Spam came the nearest to approximating the porky taste of human flesh" [qtd. in Sacks 49]. How the vegetarian Theroux knows what both Spam and human flesh taste like is not revealed; perhaps he not only traveled among Spam-eaters, he partook of the dreaded meat, awakening in himself ancestral memories of feasting on human flesh in the dark, cold caves of Europe. (The Greek god Cronus devoured his own children; the Spanish artist Goya imagined and painted the gruesome scene.) Had Theroux wanted to write about real cannibals, he could have stayed at home and composed "Notable American Cannibals, from the Donner Party to Dahmer."

In *Ruling Chiefs of Hawai'i,* Kamakau gives a native account of what happened to the remains of Captain Cook. It was customary in traditional times to clean the flesh from the bones of a deceased relative or a powerful enemy and keep the bones, which contained the mana of the person. Kamakau writes: "Then they stripped the flesh from the bones of Lono [i.e., Cook]. The palms of the hands and the intestines were kept; the remains were consumed with fire. The bones Kalani'opu'u was kind enough to give to the strangers on board the ship, but some were saved by the kahunas and worshiped" (103). Some of Cook's men assumed mistakenly that because only the bones were returned, the rest of the body had been eaten; so spread the rumor that Captain Cook was a victim of cannibalism. *Ka Mooolelo Hawaii,* a native history collected by Hawaiian students at the Lāhaināluna Seminary (1838), gives an even more graphic account of Cook's fate. Some inadvertent cannibalism is attributed to the folly of youth:

> ...they took Cook's corpse with them and those of four men who had died with him up to Ka'awaloa.
>
> Then Kalani'ōpu'u sacrificed Cook; and when he had done so he stripped the flesh off the bones and the hand (palm) and the intestines—the latter for making a kind of cord.
>
> They burned his flesh. The intestines were mistakenly eaten by

some boys, Kupa, Moho'ole, and Kaiwikoko'ole. They thought they were eating dog intestines. Some of the bones were returned to the vessel. Some were kept and worshiped by the priest. (Kahananui, 174-175)

Nakuina's "O'ahunui," whether it is read as history or allegory (and it is possibly both), supports the assertion that cannibalism was antithetical to Hawaiian values; it was anathema to Kāne, a god to whom life was sacred. Nakuina attributes the introduction of cannibalism to a foreign source ("chiefs from the South Seas") and recounts the rejection of the practice. From this perspective, "O'ahunui" is the type of story, found worldwide, which reaffirms the humanity of a group by establishing the rejection of human flesh as food. Arens notes: "The Chamula Indians of Mexico provide an interesting case.... The Chamula share a common mythical structure of worldwide distribution which includes creation of humans and later their destruction for the commission of unpardonable sins. They look upon the present as the fourth re-creation, and explain the demise of the inhabitants of the first stage as being caused by their custom of eating their own children. ...cannibalism in the mythical past, as among the Chamula, often takes the form of one member of the family devouring another as the ultimate horror" (146).

Another story by Nakuina, "Nanaue, the Shark Man" (Thrum *Hawaiian Folk Tales*, 255-268) tells of the cannibalism of a half-man, half-shark, who developed an appetite for human flesh after being fed dog meat and pork by his maternal grandfather, against the command of his shark god father, Kamohoali'i. "Powerful and beneficent," the shark god was adamantly opposed to the consumption of human flesh. The cannibal shark was finally hunted down and destroyed by the people. As Arens notes of stories of cannibalism found in other cultures, "The fact that only those animals who somehow invert their own natural order, such as the renegade lion or tiger, and certain species such as the solitary nocturnal leopard or hyena, sometimes prey on humans for food strengthens the symbolic association between cannibalism and antisocial behavior" (140-141).

2. Feeding the Gods

While there is no evidence that cannibalism was ever customarily practiced in Hawai'i, Malo, Kamakau, and Ii ('I'i) give accounts of human sacrifice during the consecration of luakini—heiau for human sacrifice (Malo 159-176, Kamakau *Works*, 129-145, Ii 33-45). Human sacrifice is a kind of symbolic cannibalism, a feeding of the gods, with whom the ali'i were closely identified. The motive of human sacrifice was to gain a god's favors, particularly the war god Kū, but also the agricultural god Lono:

luakini were built when one ruling chief was "about to make war upon another independent monarch or when he heard that some other king was about to make war against him; also when he wished to make the crops flourish...." (Malo 160-161), or to bring "peace for the duration of the reign of the king" (Ii 45). According to Malo, there was an element of cannibalism during the luakini rituals: a man impersonating the god Kahōali'i (an underworld deity) "ate an eye plucked from the man whose body had been laid as an offering on the lele [a stand for sacrifices]" (174-5). A similar ritual act of consuming an eye of the man sacrificed is described by Malo as part of the Makahiki celebration in honor of the god Lono (152).

The contradiction between the abhorrence of cannibalism in everyday life and the practice of ritualistic cannibalism in a religious context may be explained, Arens believes, "by the paradox which is religion." Religion "often demands a suspension of everyday reasoning and standards," so that the abomination of cannibalism may be "transformed into the most sacred of all acts. In this way, the religious systems demonstrate their ideological superiority over other moral precepts and the human mind" (160). Arens refers the reader to the Eucharist, in which Catholics eat bread and wine that has been transubstantiated into the body and blood of Christ.

It is also possible that there were two competing ethics in pre-contact Hawai'i: one associated with the god Kāne, to whom life was sacred and human sacrifice and cannibalism, ritualistic or not, was abhorrent; and one worshiping Kū, which required human sacrifice and ritual cannibalism as necessary to obtain the favors of the gods during a war or famine or to prevent war or famine from occurring. But the reality was not that simple: in the rites at the heiau for human sacrifice, prayers were addressed to Kāne, Lono, and Kanaloa as well as Kū (Malo, "Notes to Chapter 37" ["Concerning the Luakini"] 176-187; Kamakau *Works* 143; Ii 37-38). At the time of contact with the West, the kahuna included all four major gods when asking to have his prayers for an ali'i answered.

3. Taputapuātea

The practice of human sacrifice is said to have been brought to Hawai'i by the priest Pā'ao, who came from Wawau (Borabora) and 'Ūpolu (Taha'a), two islands near Ra'iātea in Tahiti Nui. (Thrum *More Hawaiian Folk Tales* 46-52; Kamakau *Tales* 3-5, 97-100; Pukui *Folktales* 68-73). Pā'ao was notorious for his cruelty. He was a priest of Kū, the war god; his brother Lonopele was a priest of Lono (Tahitian Ro'o), the agricultural god. Both had farm lands, rich in sweet potato, taro, and banana. One day, Lonopele accused Pā'ao's son of stealing fruits from his land; Pā'ao denied the accusation and offered to cut open the stomach of his son to search for evidence to settle the dispute. Lonopele declined to pursue the case, but Pā'ao, incensed by the accusation, cut open his son anyway, and found nothing. He swore revenge against his brother for his son's death. He built a canoe to leave his homeland and placed a kapu on the canoe. When his brother's son came by and slapped the side of the canoe, Pā'ao had him put to death for breaking the kapu. Pā'ao then departed for Hawai'i. Lonopele sent stormy winds to sink his brother's canoe, but Pā'ao was saved by two fish—the 'opelu and the aku, which calmed the seas. (These two fish became sacred to his family, kapu during their spawning seasons; at the lifting of the kapu on aku fishing toward the end of Makahiki festival, the eye of an aku fish was eaten along with the eye of a human sacrifice.)

Pā'ao landed on Hawai'i Island and founded three heiau—Waha'ula in the district of Puna, Mo'okini in Kohala, and Hikiau in Kealakekua Bay, Kona. All three heiau were luakini, where human sacrifice was practiced.

According to one Tahitian tradition, the practice of human sacrifice in Polynesia originated at a marae (temple) called Taputapuātea in the district of Opoa, on the island of Ra'iātea, 120 miles WNW of Tahiti.

Ra'iātea, the largest and highest of the leeward islands of Tahiti Nui, might have been one of the first islands in Central Polynesia to be discovered and settled by voyagers from Sāmoa or Tonga. The first marae in the district of Opoa, about half a mile inland along a streambed, was called Vaeara'i, or "Foot of Heaven," which Handy interprets as meaning "The [first] settlement of the ari'i, or ruling chiefs," who claimed descent from the gods (Handy *History and Culture in the Society Islands* 84). The district of Opoa, eventually became the religious center of Polynesia. Buck writes, "The priests at Opoa gathered the warp of myth and the weft of history together and wove them into the textile of theology" (87). The general pattern of Polynesian religion was developed: a Sky Father Ātea (Wākea) and an Earth Mother Papa were said to have given birth to children who had special functions:

Tāne (Hawaiian: Kāne), forestry and craftsmanship
Tū (Hawaiian: Kū), war
Ro'o (Hawaiian: Lono), peace and agriculture
Ta'aroa (Hawaiian: Kanaloa), marine affairs and fishing
Ra'a (Hawaiian: La'amaomao), wind and weather

Houses of learning were established, where scholars could study religion, genealogies, heraldry, and oratory, as well as astronomy, geography, and navigation. Scholars came to Opoa to acquire this knowledge, and voyagers spread the knowledge to other islands, including Hawai'i. Ra'iātea became a center of voyaging because its lagoon provided safe anchorage and its forests were abundant in trees for canoe-building. The great navigator and explorer Hiro went to this island in search of trees for his famous canoe *Hohoio* ("Interloper") (Henry 546-552).

After the pantheon of gods was spread to newly discovered islands throughout eastern Polynesia, the god Ta'aroa rose supreme over all the other gods in Ra'iātea. Ta'aroa may have been established as the supreme god after his priests were successful in ending a prolonged drought, which caused much suffering among the people. The priests ended the drought through human sacrifice:

> Before the flood, when Maui the priest built marae and established priests in all the regions, the world was luxuriant and the people were in favor with the gods, so that they had no need of human sacrifices. But there came a time when there was great drought and excessive heat in Havai'i (Ra'iātea).... And the king, moved to pity for his people told the priests to pray and present offerings to Ta'aroa that they might regain his favor and obtain rain from heaven to restore the land. The priests reflected and said, "We must have a pa'i-atua service," which was done with offerings of lean pigs, fish, and bird feathers, having no fruit or other things [because of the drought] to present with them.
>
> [When these offerings had no effect] the King said, "We must humble ourselves before God; we must tremble with fear! Let us offer a man as a tapu (pledge or sacrifice) to atone for unintentional offenses and regain God's favor in this our great distress." So the priest slew a man and offered him at the shrine of Ta'aroa, and soon clouds gathered in the sky, and rain fell and restored the land to its former flourishing condition. Thus it was shown that the gods liked human flesh, which was called te avae roroa (long-legged fish).... (Henry 196)

After the success of human sacrifice in ending this drought, the ritual was apparently adopted by the war god 'Oro as well. 'Oro was the son of Ta'aroa, and Taputapuātea became the marae for his worship. 'Oro was represented by an image woven of sennit "in the shape of a man, two or three feet long, and covered with red and yellow plumage"; the image was adorned with "a girdle of red feathers" (Henry 121), symbolic of the god's great mana. Just as the agriculture god Ro'o (Lono) received offerings of fruits, and the fishing god offerings of fish, the war god received offerings of corpses of slain enemies—the fruits of war: "To Taputapuātea...were taken most of the heads of warriors, who were decapitated as they lay dead or wounded upon the battlefield. The heads were cleaned and closely stacked in rows in the crevices and nooks of the marae, where contrasted with the background of stones, they produced a terrifying sight" (Henry 121). The sacrifices to the war god were invariably men, though female victims of black magic or war were sometimes offered to 'Oro's daughter Toi-mata (Henry 198). Handy describes the terrifying practice of obtaining sacrifices from the general population (suggesting that human sacrifice eventually was practiced in peace time to prevent war and famine?):

> The warriors of the chief would go out, sometimes by canoe, sometimes by land, going to this or that house through the length and breadth of Ra'iātea. Coming to a house they would inquire, "Aita te hue parari?" (Is the gourd not broken?) If an inmate replied, "No," the household was spared; but if the reply was, "Yes," the householder was thrust through with a spear and with all the members of his family, was taken back to the marae. Only adults were impaled; children had a spear thrust through one ear and were dragged in the water behind the canoe. Those that did not drown before they reached the Po ["Darkness"; the area surrounding the marae] were killed at the marae. The skulls of the sacrifices were thrown into the great box-like platform. (*History and Culture in the Society Islands* 89)

Malo describes a similar method for obtaining a sacrifice for the dedication of a luakini heiau: if no ulua (crevalle) could be caught for a ceremony called "ka-papa-ulua," a human corpse was substituted: "... [The priests] returned to land and went from one house to another, shouting out to the people within and telling them some lie or other and asking them to come outside. If any one did come out, him they killed, and thrusting a hook in his mouth, carried him to the heiau. If there were many people in the house, they resisted and thus escaped" (172-173).

Taputapuātea eventually became the meeting place for the Te Fa'a Tau Aroha—The Friendly Alliance, whose members worshiped 'Oro (Henry 119-127). On an appointed day, the canoes from other islands in this oceanic alliance entered the sacred pass of Te Ava Moa, bringing human sacrifices with them to increase the mana of 'Oro as well as to secure a portion of that mana for their own gods.

On the deck of each canoe were laid out human corpses, alternating with crevalle, shark, and turtle. The sacrifices were brought ashore and the visiting gods were taken to the holy enclosure of the marae, where 'Oro was waiting to receive them. 'Oro was unwrapped from his red and yellow feathers; the lesser gods from the outer islands, each in turn, were unwrapped and presented by their owners to 'Oro. Each god offered a new feather amulet or loose feathers to 'Oro in exchange for some of his. The gifts from 'Oro were meant to add mana to the lesser gods or to replace feathers lost in battle. New gods (i.e. their images) were consecrated with gifts from 'Oro. After the exchange of gifts, the gods were re-wrapped and taken to the house of sacred treasures, which was 'Oro's home. From there, the gods of the outer islands were transported to their canoes for the voyage home (Henry 119-127; 157-177).

At the time of these sacred rites, which lasted three days, kapu (prohibitions) were enforced—a hush came over the land; no fires could be lit, no food eaten. (Compare Kamakau's descriptions of the restrictions during the luakini ceremonies in Hawai'i: "There must be absolute silence; no fire could be lighted, no tapa beater sounded. A solemn stillness must prevail when the 'ōhi'a ko procession [carrying timber to manufacture the houses and images for the heiau] passed along" [*Works* 137-138]; "There should be no sound of bird, no hoot of owl, no cry of night heron, no quack of duck, no red glow at sea or of any object in the sky, no shooting star, no thunder or lighting as the kahuna went there with deliberate step, gradually leaving off his audible praying and giving the prayer to ward off evil influences" [141].)

After the ceremony at the marae was over, the kapu were lifted, and the people could breathe freely and eat again. A feast in honor of 'Oro was held on the marae, and the visiting gods were invited to partake of 'Oro's hospitality. Then the priests joined the people outside of the sacred grounds for another feast. Early the following day, the human sacrifices were buried. The corpses rendered the marae even more sacred (Henry 124-5).

4. Kapukapuākea

Variants of the place names Ra'iātea and Taputapuātea are found in Waialua, on O'ahu's north shore: Laniākea (Ra'iātea) is a beach area and famous surfing spot just north of Hale'iwa; and Kapukapuākea (Taputapuātea) was a heiau located near Hale'iwa on the east side of Kaiaka Bay. This heiau was apparently built much earlier than the luakini built by Pā'ao on Hawai'i Island. Pā'ao came to Hawai'i in the reign of Lanakawai, 43 generations after Papa and Wākea. Kapukapuākea is mentioned 18 generations earlier, in the genealogical chant of Kapawa, whose caul was placed at Kapukapuākea.

Could these places on O'ahu's north shore have been named by a group of Polynesian voyagers from Ra'iātea, who brought the practice of human sacrifice to Hawai'i before the time of Pā'ao? And could the stories of cannibalism associated with Waialua be connected to the ritualistic cannibalism of human sacrifice—victims captured by warriors of the invading chiefs and served on altars as food for their gods? One tradition of a man-eating chief called Kalō'aikanaka, who arrived on Kaua'i with a band of strangers and later fled to O'ahu, associates the cannibalism with "religious feasts" (Beckwith 342), rather than the secular banquets depicted in Nakuina's "O'ahunui."

A tradition of the rejection of human sacrifice on O'ahu is found in the story of the mō'ī Ma'ilikūkahi, who was born at Kūkaniloko to Pua'a-a-Kahuoi and Nononui. Ma'ilikūkahi was a descendant of the voyaging chief Mo'ikeha, through Mo'ikeha's son Ho'okamali'i and grandson

Kaha'i. He appears five generations after Kaha'i in the Nana'ulu genealogy, 37 generations after Papa and Wākea. Ma'ilikūkahi replaced Haka, a descendant of Mo'ikeha's older brother Kumuhonua, as mō'ī of O'ahu. Ma'ilikūkahi and Haka are archetypal chiefs, one pono (just), and one hewa (unjust). Such pairs turn up in Hawaiian genealogies whenever a change of rule takes place, a good chief deposing a bad one. The stories told about the two chiefs justify the change and serve to warn future chiefs that only through just rule could they remain in authority. Haka, like the cannibal king O'ahunui, was hewa—he was "stingy" and "did not take care of the chiefs and people. Because of this, the chiefs rebelled against him.... Haka took refuge in the pu'u kana Waewae, the fortified hill at Kawiwi there in Līhu'e." He was betrayed by his watchman, who allowed the rebels into the stronghold at night. "The rebelling chiefs and warriors came up, crowding thickly into the stronghold. Haka was the only person killed" (Kamakau *Tales* 53-54). Mā'ilikūkahi was consecrated to rule O'ahu at the heiau of Kapukapuākea, his navel cord symbolically cut and the ceremony of circumcision reenacted "to cleanse and purify him" (Kamakau *Tales* 54). He was famous for making O'ahu safe, productive, prosperous, and populous. He divided up the land, assigned a chief to each, commanded the chiefs to "cultivate the land, raise pigs and dogs and fowl," and not to steal from each other on penalty of death. He took under his care all the first-born sons of his kingdom and raised them as his own: "The chiefs and commoners loved him for his great aloha for their children" (55). He is said to have ended the practice of human sacrifices seven generations before Pā'ao re-introduced it to Hawai'i: Mā'ilikūkahi "did not sacrifice men in the heiau and luakini. That was the way of the Kūkaniloko chiefs. There were no sacrificial heiau, po'o kanaka ["human heads"], there" (Kamakau *Tales* 56).

No trace of the heiau of Kapukapuākea remains today. In the aftermath of the abolition of the kapu system (1819), the Hawaiian gods were repudiated and the heiau and images of the gods were destroyed. (Not without some resistance from some of the ali'i and kahuna; see "Abolition of the Tabus under Liholiho" in Kamakau's *Ruling Chiefs* 219-228 for an account of the resistance.) By the end of the 19th century, most of the native Hawaiian population—the estimated five percent that survived epidemic diseases introduced by colonists and immigrants—had been converted to Christianity by American missionaries. The stones of Kapukapuākea were perhaps used for road-building or other public works. Christians and converts no doubt justified their destruction of the old religion and heiau by pointing to the human sacrifices that took place at luakini heiau. But human sacrifice was hardly the essence of Hawaiian culture. Human sacrifice was practiced to prevent the devastation of wars or famine; and Ma'ilikūkahi rejected and banned the practice even for that purpose. He was able to bring peace and prosperity to his kingdom by good management of people and resources instead.

In everyday life, the kanaka maoli valued generosity, productivity and procreation, good health, love of children, respect for elders, and long life. They prayed to Kāne, the god of life-giving water, for long life:

ā kaniko'o ("until cane-tapping"; i.e. walking with a cane)
ā haumaka 'iole ("until bleary-eyed like a rat")
ā pala lauhala ("until the hala leaf dries")

ā kau i ka puaneane ("until the extremity of life is reached"; "when universal decay is coming on, yet the person is free from pain or suffering"; "a world of light and life"—"he ao malama, he wahi e ola mau loa"; "eternity"—Andrews.)

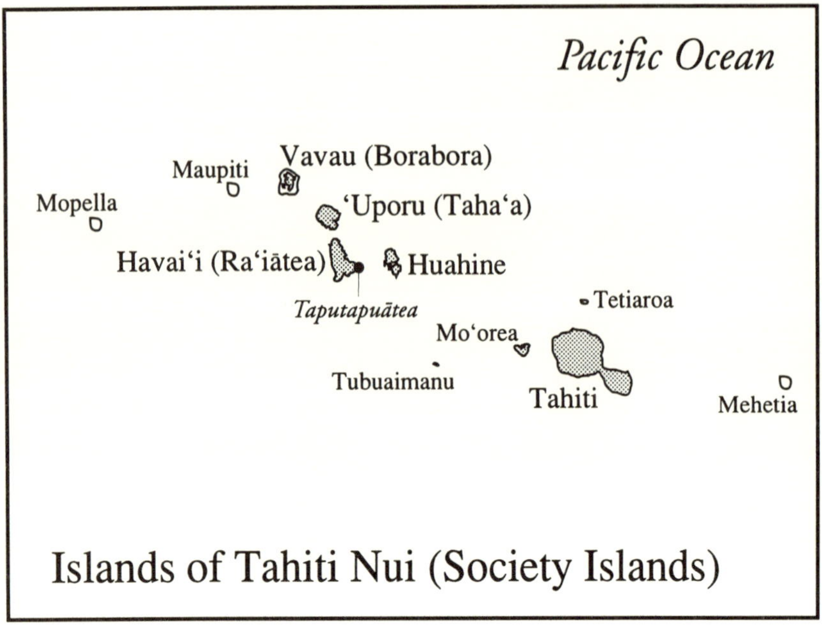
Pacific Ocean
Vavau (Borabora)
Maupiti
Mopella
'Uporu (Taha'a)
Havai'i (Ra'iātea)
Huahine
Taputapuātea
Tetiaroa
Mo'orea
Tubuaimanu
Tahiti
Mehetia
Islands of Tahiti Nui (Society Islands)

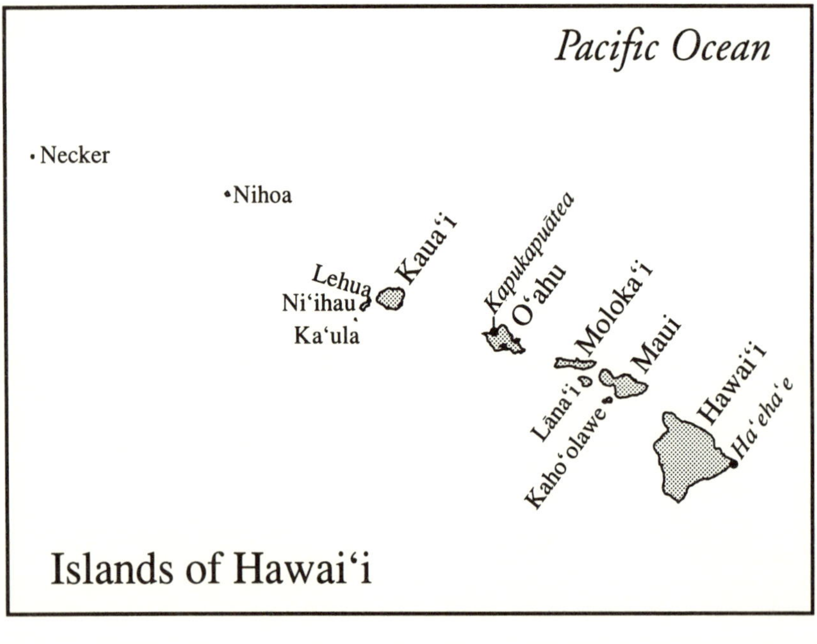
Pacific Ocean
Necker
Nihoa
Kaua'i
Lehua
Ni'ihau
Ka'ula
Kapukapuātea
O'ahu
Moloka'i
Maui
Lāna'i
Kaho'olawe
Hawai'i
Ha'eha'e
Islands of Hawai'i

He Mele no Kāne / A Song of Life

The god Kāne is said to have come from Kahiki:

Holo mai Kāne mai Kahiki
Holo a iʻa iloko o ke kai
Ke kekele ʻau i ka moana
O Haumea ke kaikuahine
O Kanaloa ia me Kāne.

Here comes Kāne from Kahiki
Coming like a fish in the sea,
Gliding through the ocean currents
Haumea the sister
And Kanaloa are with Kāne.

(Kamakau *People* 68)

The genealogy of Kāne is variously given in Hawaiian traditions. Kamakau says Kāne, along with Lono and Kū, was the god of human creation; Papa and Wākea appear twenty-eight generations later. According to Pakui, "a lineal descendant of historians from the the very darkest ages," Wākea lived with Papa and gave birth to Kāne and Kanaloa (Buck 252). "The Kumulipo states that Kāne and Kanaloa were born together as the children of Kumuhonua (Foundation-of-the-earth) and Haloiho (Peer-beneath). Nineteen pairs later, in the same list, Wākea appears" (Buck 252).

Beckwith says Kāne was an ancestor of both chiefs and commoners, and worshiped by all social classes (*Hawaiian Mythology* 42), suggesting there was a classless society before the society became stratified into social classes. The different classes of Hawaiians are said to have come into existence in the generation of Papa and Wākea: the aliʻi traced their ancestry to Wākea; the kāhuna came from Līhauʻula; and the makaʻāinana from Makuʻu. These three brothers were sons of Kahiko Luamea and Kūpūlanakehau (Kamakau *Tales* 35; in the Hawaiʻi Loa tradition, the chiefs and priests are said to be descended from Kūnuiākea, a son of Hawaiʻi Loa; commoners from Makaliʻi, one of Hawaiʻiloa's navigators.)

That Kāne, Kū, and Lono were replacing the earth mother Papa and the sky father Wākea as the source of life and creation suggests a male-dominated pantheon was evolving to supplant an older balance between the male and the female gods. Kāne, whose name means "male" and "man," came to be paired with other male gods (Kāne and Kū, or Kāne and Kanaloa) or joined by Kamakau and Kepelino in a trinity with Kū and Lono, rather than with a female deity (cf. Kū and Hina, or Papa and Wākea).

Kāne worship was simple, "without human sacrifice or laborious ritual. As such, it was unlike Kū worship, which was "highly ritualistic and involved human sacrifice" (Beckwith 46), or Lono worship, which was ritualized in the Makahiki festival. Although Kāne was sometimes named in prayers to Kū and Lono during rituals at the heiau, offerings and prayers to him were also made in a less formal setting, at a family altar called Pōhaku-o-Kāne ("Stone of Kāne"):

> ...a conical stone from a foot to eight feet in height, plain or with slight carving, and planted about with ti plant, where members of a family went to pray to their ʻaumākua and ask forgiveness for the broken tapu to which they ascribed any trouble that had come upon them. Here they sought protection from their family god with offerings and prayer. They came early in the morning, chewed ʻawa while a pig was baking, and, when all was ready, ate under tapu, leaving no remnants and clearing away all rubbish. (Beckwith 46-47)

Kāne is said to have brought kalo, the main food crop, and other cultivated plants (coconuts, breadfruit, ʻawa, and wauke) to Hawaiʻi (Beckwith 62). A prayer to accompany an offering to Kāne of kalo and ʻawa leaves goes as follows (Kamakau 35):

E kūlia, e ikūmaumaua ē ke akua,
Ē Kāne, ē Kāneikawaiola;
Eia ka lūʻau, ka lauʻawa mua o ka ʻai a kakou;
E hoʻi e ʻai ke akua;
E ʻai hoʻi koʻu ʻohana,
E ʻai ka puaʻa,
E ʻa ka ʻilio.
E ola hoʻi aʻu i ko pulapula,
I mahiʻai, i lawaiʻa, i kūkulu hale,
A kanikoʻo, haumakaʻiole, a palalauhala,
A kau i ka puaaneane;
O kau ola ka hoʻi ia.
ʻAmama, ua noa; lele wale aku la hoʻi.

Pause and receive thanks, O god.
O Kāne, O Kāne-of-the-water-of-life;
Here is the taro leaf, our first ʻawa leaf;

Turn back and eat, O god;
May my family also eat,
The pigs eat,
The dogs eat.
Grant success to me, your offspring,
In farming, in fishing, in house-building,
Until I am bent with age, blear-eyed as a rat, yellow as a
    hala leaf,
And reach advanced old age;
This is the life that is yours to grant.
'Amama, the kapu is freed; the prayer has gone on its way.

Kāne was the god of life, associated with fertility, good health, longevity—and life-giving water. "'Life is sacred to Kāne (ua kapu ke ola na Kāne)', was the saying'" (Beckwith 46).

"He Mele no Kāne / A Song of Kāne," a six-stanza chant from Kaua'i, celebrates the god Kāne and his life-giving waters (Emerson *Unwritten Literature* 257-59). Each of the six stanzas begins with the question "Where is the water of Kāne?" The six answers to the question come in pairs of opposites, a common organizing device in Hawaiian chant:

Stanza 1: In the East, toward the rising sun.
Stanza 2: In the West, toward the setting sun.

Stanza 3: In the mountains.
Stanza 4: At sea.

Stanza 5: In the atmosphere above.
Stanza 6: In the ground below.

The three pairs of opposites convey completeness and ubiquity. Kāne brings water to his worshipers from all parts of the cosmos. The structural devices of the chant—the pairs of opposites, the repetition, the parallel elements in each stanza—suggest a world of balance, fullness, and order. Within this world, life is abundant, because water is everywhere, in so many sources, in all directions:

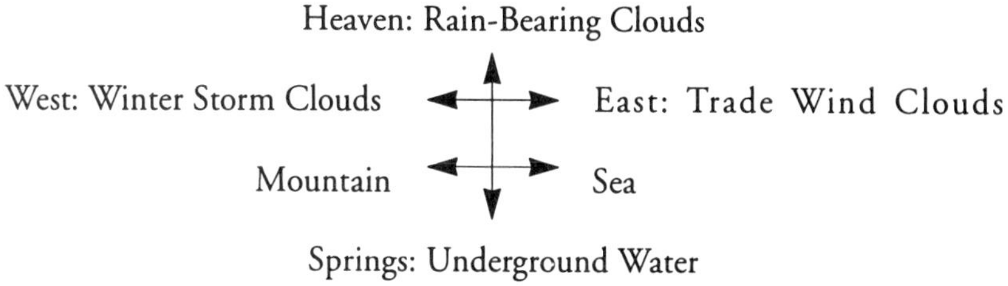

The balance and order of the nature was dynamic. The rising and setting sun, mentioned in the first two stanzas, are symbolic of life and death, of the passing of the seasons of Ho'oilo, with its winter storms, and Kau, with its trade wind clouds. Stanzas three and four suggest the hydrological cycle: water from the mountains flow down to the sea; water from the ocean rises up into the atmosphere in the form of clouds. The water of Kāne comes from the sky above, falling as rain; and from the ground below, gushing up in springs. The rising of underground water in the last stanza of the poem takes the reader back to the rising sun in the first stanza, giving the chant a cyclical structure. The images are linked metaphorically: the water welling up from the earth suggests rebirth, like the sun emerging from the base of heaven each morning; or like kalo planted in the rainy season of Ho'oilo, nourished by the rain, its edible root forming in the dark, wet ground, its leaves unfurling upward into the bright sunlight of Nana (April; from 'Inana, "to grow active, to animate, to come to life"), at the beginning of Kau, the season of growth.

Stanza 1: He Mele no Kāne

He ui, he nīnau,
E ui aku ana au iā 'oe:
Aia i hea ka wai a Kāne?
Aia i ka hikina a ka lā,
Puka I Ha'eha'e,
Aia i laila ka wai a Kāne.

A query, a question,
I ask you:
Where is the water of Kāne?
There where the sun rises,
Emerging at Ha'eha'e,
There is the water of Kāne.

The opening stanza of "He Mele no Kāne" points to the east to answer the question, "Where is the water of Kāne?": the water of Kāne is found beyond the eastern horizon, and is carried to the islands in clouds on Ka Moa'e—the ENE trade winds, which dominate the summer season of Kau.

Stanza 2: He Mele no Kāne

E ui aku ana au iā 'oe:

Aia i hea ka wai a Kāne?
Aia i Kaulana ka lā,
I ke pae ʻōpua i ke kai,
Ea mai ana ma Nihoa,
Ma ka mole mai o Lehua,
Aia i laila ka wai a Kāne.

I ask you:
Where is the water of Kāne?
There where the sun sets,
In the cloud banks lined up at sea,
Approaching from Nihoa,
From the base of Lehua,
There is the water of Kāne.

The second stanza points toward the setting sun, the direction from which cold fronts come during Hoʻoilo preceded by banks of clouds at the horizon called ʻōpua, harbingers of rain:

"Aia ka wai i ka maka o ka ʻōpua." / "Water is in the face of the ʻōpua" (Pukui *ʻŌlelo,* No. 55).

"Ola i ka wai a ka ʻōpua." / "There is life in the water from the ʻōpua" (Pukui *ʻŌlelo,* No. 2483).

In Kona, on the west side of Hawaiʻi Island, the appearance of ʻōpua over the ocean to the west promises rain: "Māmā Kona i ka wai kau mai i ka maka o ka ʻōpua." / "Kona is relieved, knowing that there will be no drought, when the clouds promise rain." (Pukui *ʻŌlelo,* No. 2134). In one story, Kāne is said to have come from Kuaihelani on an "ao ʻōpua," an ʻōpua cloud (Pukui *Legend of Kawelo*), suggesting that such clouds were seen as canoes in which Kāne brought life-giving water to Hawaiʻi.

Malo gives the following description of ʻōpua: "If clouds stood in rows (lālani) encircling the horizon (pōʻai), close to the base of the sky (kumu o ka lani), they were called ʻōpuʻa. There were many kinds of ʻōpua, each named according to its appearance. If the leaves [lau] of the ʻōpua are hina (slanting down, suggesting rain beneath the clouds), it might indicate wind or a storm, but if the leaves stand upright (kūpono), calm weather" (translated from Malo *Ka Moolelo Hawaii* 11). Fishermen and sailors observed the ʻōpua to determine the weather for the day: "Noho no ke kanaka a ka lā mālie; kau ka ipu hōkeo a ka lawaiʻa; nānā ana i ka ʻōpua" / "A man waits for a calm day; he puts down his gourd with his fishing gear and looks at the horizon clouds" (Pukui *ʻŌlelo,* No. 2328).

Stanza 3: He Mele no Kāne

E ui aku ana au iā ʻoe:
Aia i hea ka wai a Kāne?
Aia i ke kuahiwi, i ke kualono
I ke awāwa, i ke kahawai,
Aia i laila ka wai a Kāne.

I ask you:
Where is the water of Kāne?
There on the mountain, on the ridge,
In the gulch, in the stream,
There is the water of Kāne.

The third stanza of "He Mele no Kāne" points to the mountains as a source of the water of Kāne. The rains fill mountain dikes with water, and the water seeps out and flows down, from the highest mountains (kuahiwi) and ridges (kualono), into ravines (awāwa) and streams (kahawai) to the sea, providing drinking water and irrigating loʻi kalo on its way.

Stanza 4: He Mele no Kāne

E ui aku ana au iā ʻoe:
Aia i hea ka wai a Kāne?
Aia i kai, i ka moana
I ke kualau, i ke ānuenue,
I ka pūnohu, i ka uakoko,
I ka ʻālewalewa;
Aia i laila ka wai a Kāne.

I ask you:
Where is the water of Kāne?
Over the near-shore sea, over the far sea,
in the wind-blown rain at sea, in the rainbow,
in the reddish billowing cloud, in the low red rainbow,
in the low hanging clouds,
There is the water of Kāne.

Stanza four points toward the sea to find the water of Kāne, over the near-shore sea, or kai, and the deep ocean, or moana, where the various atmospheric forms of Kāne are found—rain, rainbows, and red clouds:

1. *Kualau*—The wind-driven rain at sea, as opposed to ʻawa, rain

confined to the mountains (Malo 14). Pukui-Elbert defines *Kualau* as "a shower accompanied by a seawind" and illustrates the meaning with two lines from a chant "ē ke kualau, ka ua nū hele ma ka moana"—"rain moaning over the open sea." Andrews defines it as "a strong wind; a gale of wind; wind and rain upon the ocean ("he ua me ka makani ma ka moana"), suggesting squalls at sea, thunderclouds, with strong down drafts.

2. *Ānuenue*—the rainbow; a mix of rain and sunlight, two forms of Kāne.

3. *Pūnohu*—Emerson glosses "pūnohu" as "a red luminous cloud" (*Unwritten Literature* 258, footnote a) and translates it "piled-up mist-wraith." Pukui and Korn translate "ka pūnohu a Kāne" as "the rising reddish mist of Kāne" (54). Pukui-Elbert define punōhu as "a rainbow lying close to the earth," or as a verb, "to rise, as smoke or mist; to billow out, as a ship's sail; to spread out, as a cloud." Andrews gives "to arise or ascend, as smoke"; "to make a white appearance as the sails of a ship quickly set"; or the related, punonohu: "to swell out, to be large like the sails of a ship." The image is of a cloud suffused with reddish sunlight, billowing up, with a misty rain falling. "A rainbow with red colors predominating" was called "Kāne's red perch" ("Haka 'ula a Kāne"—Pukui *'Ōlelo*, No. 415); "haka" was "a perch for a bird"; or "a rack on which water gourds might be hung" (Pukui-Elbert). Kepelino gives a more specific definition: "The haka was a high perch made in the house for the worship of the god Kāne" (22).

4. *Ua-koko*—"Literally, 'blood-rain,' a term applied to a rainbow when lying near the ground" (Emerson *Unwritten Literature* 258). Andrews defines "uakoko" as "a cloud standing erect and having different colors, somewhat like a rainbow." Pukui-Elbert: "Reflection of rainbow colors in the clouds."

5. *'Ālewalewa*—"floating, buoyant, suspended, hanging"; Malo says "ho'olewalewa" refers to "a cloud hung low in the sky" ("ho'okokoke," "to draw near") (12). "An Ancient Prayer / He Pule Kahiko" (Fornander, Vol. V, 519) associates 'ālewalewa with the rainbow, rain, and wind:

Iho mai ka 'ālewalewa me ka ānuenue,
Hele 'ino ka ua me ka makani...

The hanging clouds and the rainbow descend
The stormy rain and wind follow...

Clouds and rain were essential to the life of the land, and the three gods of Kamakau's and Kepelino's trinity—Kāne, Kū, and Lono—all had cloud forms. Kāne is addressed as Kāne-i-ke-ao-lani (heavenly cloud)

Kāne-i-ka-maka-o-ka-'ōpua (the eye of the horizon cloud), Kāne-i-ka-'ōpua (the horizon cloud), Kāne-i-ka-ao, the floating cloud (Beckwith 59). Kū is addressed as Kū-ke-ao-loa (Kū of the long cloud) and Kū-ke-ao-poko (Kū of the short cloud) (Kamakau *People* 58). Lono is addressed as "A long cloud, a short cloud, / A watchful cloud, / An overlooking cloud; in the heavens" (Beckwith 31).

A special cloud form associated with Kane was called Kānehūnāmoku, the hidden island of Kāne, a floating island that moves on the ocean like a cloud. It was considered one of the Hawaiian Islands. Kāne and Kanaloa lived on this island with the spirits of their faithful worshipers, who came there after death. The floating island was an earthly paradise, where food was always abundant, where there was no labor or death. "Ka waiola a Kāne," "the life-giving waters of Kāne," which could restore a person's health or life, is found on the island (Beckwith 73-74). "This land floats in the sea and appears at dawn at the eastern points of various islands. It touches one island and goes on to the next" (Kepelino 189). Families who worship Kāne have reportedly waited for the island to appear, so they could go on it, though according to another tradition, no human being was allowed onto the island, only spirits. (William Hyde Rice tells the story of a pious worshiper of Kāne, Makuakaumana, who was allowed to live there for a while [116-132].)

Stanza 5: He Mele no Kāne

E ui aku ana au iā 'oe:
Aia i hea ka wai a Kāne?
Aia i luna ka wai a Kāne,
I ke 'ōuli, i ke ao 'ele'ele,
I ke ao panopano,
I ke ao pōpolo-hua mea a Kāne,
Aia i laila ka wai a Kāne.

I ask you:
Where is the water of Kāne?
There in the sky above is the water of Kāne,
In the portents of the sky, in the black clouds,
In the thickening clouds,
In the dark purple cloud of Kāne,
There is the water of Kāne.

The fifth stanza of "He Mele no Kāne" points upward (iluna) to the water of Kāne in the thick, dark rising cumulonimbus clouds, the thunderheads that bring strong wind and heavy rain. The clouds are seen as a sign of the god's approach ('ōuli). He appears first as ao 'ele'ele, black clouds, and ao panopano, thick, dark clouds. "Pano" also suggests "sacred," "mysterious," "unapproachable," applied to "very high chiefs believed to be of divine descent" (Pukui-Elbert). This suggestion of divinity and sacredness becomes explicit in the next image in which the dark cloud is said to belong to Kāne, as a child to parent: "ao pōpolo-hua mea a Kāne." Emerson translates "ao pōpolo-hua mea" as "the black-mottled sacred cloud of the gods"; Pukui-Elbert translates a parallel term applied to the ocean ("kai pōpolo-hua mea a Kāne") as "the purplish-blue, reddish brown sea of Kāne" (from "pōpolo-hua," "purplish blue, as the sea; dark as a bruise" and "mea," "reddish brown")." An adjective (rare) similar to "pōpolo-hua mea" is "pōlolohuamea," translated by Pukui-Elbert as "dark, dense, distant," and by Andrews as "green and far off, as the sea at a great distance."

Stanza 6: He Mele no Kāne

E ui aku ana au iā 'oe:
Aia i hea ka wai a Kāne?
Aia i lalo, I ka honua, I ka wai hu,
I ka wai kau a Kāne me Kanaloa,
He waipuna, he wai e inu,
He wai e mana, he wai e ola,
E ola nō, 'eā!

I ask you:
Where is the water of Kāne?
There in the ground below, in the water gushing up,
in the water made by Kāne and Kanaloa,
a freshwater spring, water to drink,
Water to give strength, water to give life,
Bless us with life!

The final stanza of "He Mele no Kāne" points downward (ilalo) to the water of Kāne in the ground. Kāne is often paired with the god Kanaloa and associated with springs. Kāne is said to have been dark, with curly hair and thick lips; Kanaloa was tall and fair (Beckwith *Hawaiian Mythology* 63). The two gods, guardians of the purity of freshwater, created springs on various islands after arriving in Hawai'i. They stopped first on Kaho'olawe, then continued on:

> ... the two went to Kahikinui, Maui, where they opened up the fishpond of Kanaloa at Lua-la'i-lua, and from them came the water of

> Kou at Kaupō. They caused the deaths of the unholy priests (kāhuna ʻaiā) at Koʻina at Kīkoʻo in Kīpahulu and of the grandchild of Waianu for defiling drinking water. They broke open rocks so that water would gush forth—sweet, flowing water—at Waiheʻe and at Kahakuloa on Maui, on Lānaʻi, at Waiakāne in Punakou on Molokaʻi, and at Kawaihoa on Oʻahu. This they did throughout the islands. (*Tales* 112)

A version of this Kāne tradition, told by Annie Harris and recorded by Pukui, is localized on Oʻahu (Pukui *Legend of Kawelo* 112-115): Kāne and Kanaloa came to Hawaiʻi from Kuaihelani, "one of the twelve mythical islands in the clouds controlled by the god Kāne and inhabited by his followers." They arrived at Hanauma Bay on Oʻahu. The area was dry, with no running streams or springs. As they traveled westward through the Kona district, whenever they wanted to refresh themselves with ʻawa (a drink made from the root of a pepper plant), Kāne created a spring by thrusting his staff into the bedrock: "many waterholes [were] made by Kāne between Hanauma and Laeʻahi [Diamond Head]." When Kāne and Kanaloa reached Waikīkī at ʻĀpuakēhau, they went swimming, then proceeded to Mōʻiliʻili and washed the sand off their feet at Papaʻakea Stream. (Kapaʻakea? this was the area makai of Mānoa valley, including Mōʻiliʻili; see the map of old Honolulu in Ii 93.) The two gods then proceeded to Makiki where Kāne created the spring at Punahou by piercing the hill of Keapapa. They visited Pūʻahuʻula in upper Mānoa Valley, the site of a spring, where the moʻo goddess Kihanuilūlūmoku lived (Pukui et al, *Place Names of Hawaii*).

Finally, the two gods reached Waiakeakua ("Water [used] by the gods," the easternmost stream in Mānoa Valley) and climbed a steep cliff, where they met Kāmehaʻikana, a goddess who could take the form of a stone, but also had the form of the breadfruit tree: "Another tree with mana was the breadfruit tree into which Haumea entered, and which then became the kingdom-seeking god Kamehaʻikana" (Kamakau, *People* 129). Kāne and Kanaloa wanted to make love to this goddess and she was smitten with love for them, but her attendant feared her mistress would die if both gods possessed her, so she threw herself in front of Kāmehaʻikana to block the way. The attendant remains there in the stream today as a stone, head down, feet up, a position of humility and sacrifice. Kāne's footprint is pointed out on a rock where he stepped. At the place where Kāne and Kanaloa stood, two mountain apple trees (ʻōhiʻa ʻai) sprang up to guard the waters.

This story brings together the male and female elements in freshwater springs in Hawaiʻi: "Kāne as spear thruster and god of gushing waters has phallic symbolism. The thruster is the male, the spring of water, which Hawaiians think of as the source of life, is the female in the generative process" (Beckwith *Hawaiian Mythology* 66). The guardians of springs, as in the story of Waiakeakua, are often female. Harris' story does not claim the spring of Waiakeakua made by Kāne, rather that he and Kanaloa found a spring there, with a guardian goddess, suggesting that the worship of female springs was already established in some rainy, wet uplands before the arrival of Kāne and Kanaloa from Kahiki.

Beckwith adds the following note to Harris' story:

> Mr. John Holani Hao of Waialua, O'ahu, thinks that this is a fanciful story and that the name [Waiakeakua] comes from the fact that only the high chiefs were allowed to use this spring; it was tapu to others. A chief would often test the courage and fidelity of a retainer by despatching him at night to fill a bottle at this spring. The trickle was so slow that water could be obtained only by using a footstalk of banana as trough. The fear of spirits abroad at night would daunt all but the bravest. The water when drawn was full of fine bubbles; if the messenger filled the bottle from another source he was always detected:—"Where are the bubbles?"

The last two lines of the last stanza in "He Mele no Kāne" list three functions of Kāne's water: ...he wai e inu, / He wai e mana, he wai e ola ("...water to drink, / Water to give strength, water to give life"). Kāne imparts his mana to drinkers of his water, giving them strength and life. While some springs were kapu to the chiefs, water was found everywhere and available to everyone; so ultimately, the worship of Kāne and his life-giving water was not limited by social class.

Two place names appear in "He Mele no Kāne": Ha'eha'e (Stanza 1) and Nihoa (Stanza 2). Ha'eha'e is a land section near Kumukahi ("First Source"); it is the easternmost point of Hawai'i, where the day begins. From the direction of the sunrise, the trade wind bring rain-bearing clouds, particularly during the summer. Somewhere beyond the eastern horizon is a source of the water. In one version of the Mo'ikeha tradition, Ha'eha'e and Kumukahi are said to be two of his crew members who were charmed by Hilo, a district north of Cape Kumukahi, and asked to be allowed to stay there. Kumukahi is said to be "represented by a red stone" (Pukui et al *Place Names*). The color red suggests power and sacredness, as well as the color of the rising sun at dawn when the sky is full of moisture-portending rain. Two of Kumukahi's wives, also represented by stones, were said to have "manipulated" the seasons, by pulling the sun back and forth between them (Pukui et al *Place Names*). This description suggests there was an astronomical station at Kumukahi, with the two female stones aligned on either side of the red stone—one alignment pointing to the sun's northernmost rising point, marking summer solstice (June 21, the longest day of the year), the other to the sun's southernmost rising point, marking winter solstice (December 22, the shortest day of the year). The movement of the sun between these two limits determine the passage of year and the seasons: Ho'oilo, the half year of cooler, wetter weather and shorter days (October to March); and Kau, the half year of hotter, drier weather and longer days (April to September).

The sun, wind, and clouds emerge from holes (puka mai) in the wall of the heavenly gourd, which is the body of the god Lono (Handy and Handy 220). Metaphorically, the sun, trade winds, and clouds are voyagers, like Kumukahi and Ha'eha'e, arriving in Hawai'i from beyond the horizon.

It rained steadily for a week in November 1996, over 13 inches in Honolulu. One band of dark clouds after another came from the west; lightning flashed, thunder resounded, and heavy drops of rain fell day and night. It reminded me of the Novembers of my childhood. Inside the bedroom I shared with my brother, under a warm cotton blanket, I listened to the rain drumming on the rooftop, dripping down on the kī plants and heliconia, splashing in the slowly rising puddles around the house. The small, old house on Kea'ahala Road in Kāne'ohe creaked as strong gusts of wind swirled under the eaves, trying to lift the roof off. I imagined being on a ship, sailing bravely through stormy seas.

The six-month dry season of Kau ended in 'Ikuwā (October-November), around the time when Makali'i (the Pleiades) appears at the ENE horizon at sunset. 'Ikuwā means "loud voice," referring to the sound of thunder and high surf that accompany the storms of Ho'oilo: "O 'Ikuwā i pohā kō'ele'ele, 'ikuwā ke kai, 'ikuwā ka hekili, 'ikuwā ka manu"—"'Ikuwā is the month which breaks out in storms, the sea roars, the thunder roars, the birds make a din" (Pukui *'Ōlelo*, No. 2390).

Cold fronts generated by low pressure systems in the North and Western Pacific move eastward along storm tracks, sweeping over the Hawaiian Islands from the direction of Nihoa, a small island WNW of Kaua'i and Lehua, a small island W of Kaua'i, just off the north tip of Ni'ihau. At the leading edge of these cold fronts are the storm clouds that bring heavy winter rainfall and strong winds: "Pa'apa'a'ina ka malo i loko o 'Ikuwā" / "The loincloth flaps in [the winds] of 'Ikuwā" (Pukui *'Ōlelo*, No. 2562).

In 1822, Ka'ahumanu and a royal party including Kaumuali'i, Liholiho, Keopuokalani and Kahekili Ke'eaumoku, visited Ni'ihau and heard chants and stories about an island called Nihoa, to the west of Kaua'i, the direction from which the winter rains came:

'Ea mai ana ke ao ua o Kona,
'Ea mai ana ma Nihoa
Ma ka mole mai o Lehua
Ua iho a pulu ke kahakai

The rain clouds of Kona come,
Approaching from Nihoa,
From the base of Lehua,
Pouring down, drenching the coast.

Intrigued, Ka'ahumanu organized an expedition and sailed in two or three boats under Captain William Sumner to visit the island. They landed on the once inhabited, but long deserted island 150 miles WNW of Kaua'i and annexed it to the Hawaiian kingdom. The waterfront area around Ka'ahumanu Street in Honolulu was named Nihoa in honor of the visit. The island was annexed to the Hawaiian Kingdom again by Kamehameha IV, who landed on the island in 1857. In 1885, Queen Lili'uokalani, with 200 excursionists, visited Nihoa on the steamer *'Iwalani*, and brought back artifacts—a stone bowl, a stone dish, a coral rubbing stone, and a coral file (Emory 8-11).

Nihoa, jutting up from the sea beyond sight of Kaua'i and Ni'ihau, is the westernmost place in this tradition of Kaua'i geography. It has come to stand for "one who bravely faces misfortune": "Kū pākū ka pali o Nihoa i ka makani"—"The cliffs of Nihoa stand strongly against the wind" (Pukui, *'Ōlelo*, No. 1924). "Nihoa" means "firmly set," or "toothed," "serrated," possibly a reference to its jagged profile; from one side, it looks like a molar, standing isolated at sea. (In Micronesia, an island seen from a departing canoe, just before the island disappears from sight is called a "tooth," and serves as a final landmark to orient the canoe on its voyage.)

Nihoa is a mile long, a quarter mile wide, and 900 feet high on its east end. It was designated a wildlife refuge by Theodore Roosevelt in 1906. It is inhabited by insects, monk seals, two species of land birds, a finch and a millerbird, found nowhere else, and numerous seabirds (terns, boobies, petrels, shearwaters, albatrosses, tropic birds, and frigate birds). Today, access is controlled by the U.S. Fish and Wildlife Service and landing, except for scientific study and cultural purposes, is prohibited.

Nihoa was once inhabited by the kanaka maoli, sometime between 1000 and 1500 A.D. About 35 house sites, 15 bluff shelters, 15 heiau, and 28 agricultural terraces have been identified on the island (Emory 12; Cleghorn 21-22). Various artifacts have also been collected, including fishhooks, sinkers, cowry shell lures, hammerstones, grindstones, adzes, and coral rubbing stone (Emory 38-50). The evidence seems to indicate permanent or semi-permanent settlement.

Living on the island would have been difficult. Surveys have discovered only three seeps of water, all contaminated with guano (Emory 12). Tava and Keale report a tradition of Ni'ihau that a spring called Waiakanohoaka provided good, sweet water (102), but this spring has not been located. The freshwater on the island comes from the estimated 20-30 inches of rain that falls annually from passing squalls (Cleghorn 26).

Archaeologists surmise that the terraces were planted with sweet potatoes, a crop requiring less water than thirsty taro. They estimate that the 12-16 acres under cultivation might have supported about 100 people (Cleghorn 25). Fish, shellfish, crabs, lobsters, turtles, and seals, as well as seabirds and their eggs, are abundant sources of food. Cleghorn speculates that the food and water supply was sufficient for subsistence, but that the lack of firewood would have created a hardship (26). The only tree on the island is the loulu palm. Archaeologist Kenneth Emory of the Bishop Museum counted 515 palms when he landed in 1923. Its fan-like leaves were used for plaiting, and its trunk could have been used for building shelters or for firewood. But if the trees were cut down for firewood, the supply would have eventually been depleted.

Without the numerous kinds of plants in the forest of the larger islands (e.g., koa, 'ōhi'a, hau, hala, olonā, wauke), the settlers could not have provided themselves with canoes, wood containers, nets, fishing line, clothing and blankets, mats, and medicines. The colony was probably supplied with these products from Kaua'i or Ni'ihau. Several gourd fragments have been found; other bowls and containers were carved from stone.

Landing on the island is difficult. High, sheer cliffs prevent landing on the east, north, and west sides; the island slopes down to the south, but the shoreline is rocky and unprotected from the surge of southerly swells. Large vessels anchor offshore, and those who wish to land have to go in on a smaller boat or swim ashore. In ancient times, small canoes could have been carried up onto the rocky coast on calm days. If the canoes used to reach the island were somehow damaged in the rough surf, the settlers would not have been able to repair their canoes with resources from the island. They would have been trapped until other canoes arrived from Ni'ihau or Kaua'i.

Partial skeletons of men, women, and children have been found on the island, and two burial sites located. The journey of spirits to the afterworld (in the west, toward the setting sun) would have been shorter from this western outpost than from the islands to the east. The name of a place on the island where spirits of the dead departed for the afterworld is still remembered: it was called Mau-loku ("Continuous falling"; Pukui et al *Place Names*).

How the island was discovered is not known—possibly by fisherman working the seas west of Kaua'i, or following seabirds to gather their feathers or eggs. Red feathers were coveted for making sacred objects, and the red-tailed tropic bird is one of the seabirds that nests on Nihoa. Polynesians traveled great distances to obtain such feathers: one Marquesan tradition tells of a 1200-mile voyage, from Hiva Oa to Rarotonga, to obtain the red feathers of a kura bird; and the voyaging chief Hema is said to have sailed back to Kahiki to obtain a girdle of red feathers for his son Kaha'i.

Once discovered, the island became a part of the economy of Ni'ihau, an island relatively limited in resources. The traditions of Ni'ihau say that the people of that island were frequent and perhaps long-term visitors to collect loulu palm wood for spears and a grass called Makiukiu, which could be used for cordage and stuffing (Tava and Keale 102).

Another motive for visiting the island is suggested by the chant of Ni'ihau describing the Kona rain clouds coming from Nihoa and soaking the west coasts of Kaua'i and Ni'ihau. Small, low islands like Ni'ihau and also the leeward coasts of high islands like Kaua'i depend on the heavy rains of annual Kona storms to bring life to their crops. But if the storms stay west or pass to the north without reaching Hawai'i, as they sometimes do, droughts and, in ancient times, famine, could occur. Could the people of Ni'ihau or leeward Kaua'i have sailed west to get closer to the source of these rain clouds or the deities who controlled them in order to pray for rain and make offerings? Water represented life and wealth in ancient Hawai'i, and such a voyage might have been worth the effort and the risk.

One hundred and fifty miles west of Nihoa is an island called Necker. This island is smaller and has even fewer resources than Nihoa. There are no trees and no soil. Yet the island is covered with some 33 heiau (Emory 59). Several stone images, the largest around 16 inches high, were found by visitors in historical times. The images look like gingerbread men—flat, neckless, with round faces, from which eyes, noses, mouths, and ears protrude (Emory 125, Illustrations XX-XXII). Who or what these images represent is unknown.

The Hawaiian name for Necker has been lost. But Teva reports that there are four names remembered on Ni'ihau of islands beyond Nihoa: Mokuakamohoali'i, Hanakaieie, Hanakeaumoe, and Ununui (103). Mokuakamohoali'i, "Island of the Shark God Kamohoali'i," is a possible name for Necker, as the largest geographical feature on this island is a bay called "Shark Bay." Kamohoali'i was the king of sharks and brother of the volcano goddess Pele. The Pele migration is said to have come from the west, with Kamohoali'i serving as the navigator.

Cleghorn suggests that in addition to going to Necker for gathering resources such as bird feathers and eggs, the visits may have had a ritualistic purpose: the heiau could have belonged to a bird cult, similar to the one on Rapa Nui (Easter Island) (61). But the heiau and statues could also have been used in rain-god worship. And as in the kachina rituals of the American Southwest, the rain deities might have been associated with ancestral spirits who return each year in the form rain clouds from their homes in the west. (The winter rains of the American Southwest come from the west, as they do in Hawai'i.) In either case, birds and rain clouds are metaphorically connected with each other in Hawaiian chant. Beckwith notes, "The cloud hanging over Ka'ula is a bird which flies before the wind:

> The blackbird begged,
> The bird of Ka'ula begged,
> Floating up there above Wa'ahila"
>
> (*The Hawaiian Romance of Laieikawai* 323).

Nihoa would have been a stop on the way to or from Necker. Annual visits to Necker during the spring and summer trade wind season could have been made, when food would have been abundant on and around Nihoa and Necker. A Ni'ihau tradition suggests such was the case: "The Ni'ihauans sailed to Nihoa in the spring, returning to Ni'ihau in the fall on the Kona winds" (Tava and Keale 102). The same sailing strategy could have taken them to Necker. After landing on Necker, prayers and offerings could have been presented to the deities. Then the pilgrims could have fished, hunted birds, collected eggs, and built or maintained heiau. When a cold front approached, the canoes could head back to Ni'ihau or Kaua'i on the southwesterly winds that precede the front or the northerly winds that follow.

Any downwind sail with the prevailing winds is a risky undertaking, because unless the wind shifts, the sail home involves tacking into the wind, something which the keel-less Polynesian canoes would have great difficulty doing. The risk is weighed against the importance of the potential benefits of going to the downwind destination. For a community dependent on farming, drought could be disastrous. If one of the sources of the life-giving waters of Kāne was westward, was it worthwhile to sail west to present offerings and prayers to a god who brought life-giving waters? For a time in Hawaiian prehistory, the answer was apparently yes; then, perhaps after dry-land taro and sweet potato cultivation in areas with limited rainfall had improved enough so that famine was no longer a seasonal threat, such voyages became unnecessary.

In June, 1994, a crew of the voyaging canoe *Hōkūleʻa* waited on Kauaʻi for the right winds to sail to Nihoa. The island was to be the target of a training voyage for navigators who would be guiding *Hōkūleʻa* and the newly-built voyaging canoe *Hawaiʻiloa* without navigational instruments on a 5,000-mile journey to Tahiti, Hiva (Marquesas Islands), and back to Hawaiʻi in the spring of 1995. The sail to Nihoa, in the direction of the setting summer sun, could be made in about a day with good trade winds; getting back was a problem. The crew would need a northeasterly wind in order to sail back; an easterly wind would force them to make long tacks to get back to Kauaʻi, which could take days.

The crew was eager to go. The sail would allow the mostly Hawaiian crew to step foot on an island that was part of their ancestors' domain and to leave a small offering of fish on shore.

But a low pressure system to the north pushed the North Pacific High away from Hawaiʻi, bringing easterly trade winds. As the crew waited, frustration mounted: Would we go? When? If not Nihoa, how about Kaʻula, or Niʻihau? Creatures of modern obligations, we did not have the time to go out to Nihoa and wait for weeks or months for the right winds to return home; we had to be back in Honolulu in a week. Nor did we have the religious inspiration to find magical red feathers, or to get closer to the mysterious source of winter rains, somewhere beyond the western horizon, to offer prayers and gifts to a rain god. Finally, the navigators abandoned the plan to go to Nihoa, and we sailed back to Oʻahu.

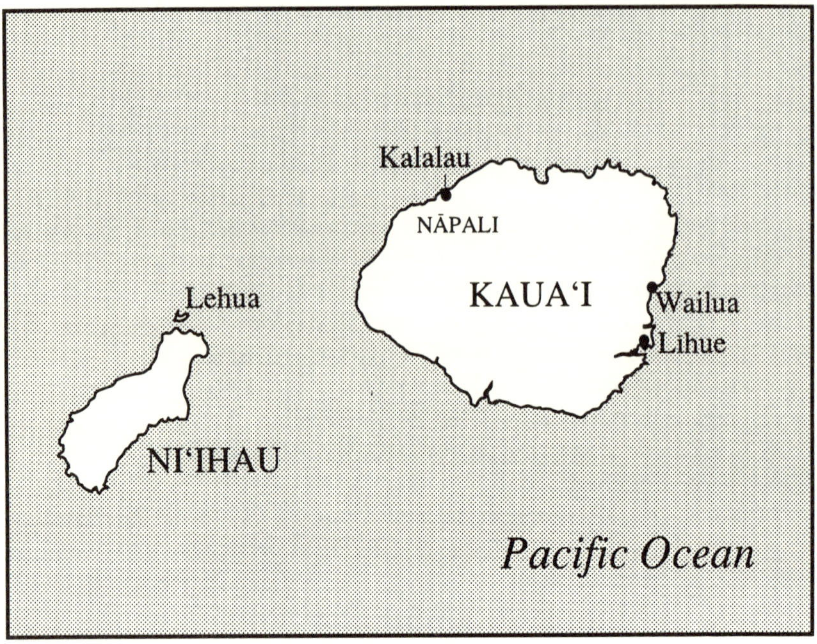
Kalalau
NĀPALI
KAUA'I
Wailua
Lihue
Lehua
NI'IHAU
Pacific Ocean

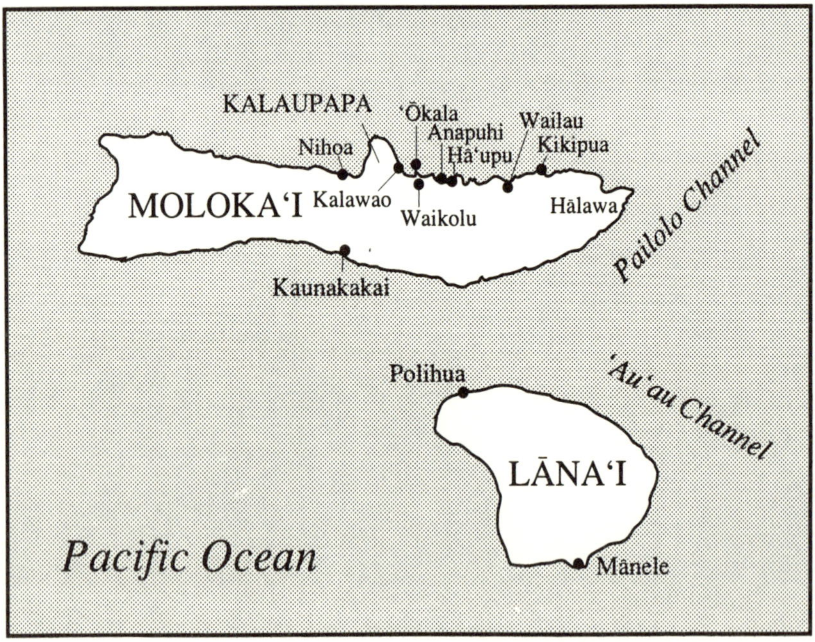
KALAUPAPA
'Ōkala
Anapuhi
Hā'upu
Wailau
Kikipua
Nihoa
MOLOKA'I
Kalawao
Waikolu
Hālawa
Kaunakakai
Pailolo Channel
Polihua
'Au'au Channel
LĀNA'I
Mānele
Pacific Ocean

A Twisted Tale: Jack London's "Koolau the Leper"

In *Our Hawaii* (1917), Charmian London cites a posthumous tribute to her husband, California writer Jack London: "Better than any one, he knew us Hawaiians." Whether "a young Hawaiian ukulele player" in San Francisco actually said this, we have only Mrs. London's word. If he did, he apparently had not read London's stories. My own impression of London is closer to the description of the archetypal Jack, visitor to the South Seas, that Herman Melville describes in *Typee*: "Jack ... invariably officiates as showman of the island on which he has settled, and having mastered a few dozen words of the language is supposed to know all about the people who speak it. A natural desire to make himself of consequence in the eyes of the strangers prompts him to lay claim to a much greater knowledge than he actually possesses....The avidity with which his anecdotes are noted down tickles his vanity, and his powers of invention increase with the credulity of his audience" (193). Melville himself told some incredible stories about the natives of Taipi in the Marquesas Islands.

Jack London visited Hawai'i three times, twice in 1904 on his way to and from Asia to cover the Russo-Japanese War and a third time for six months in 1907, arriving on his schooner *Snark* at the beginning of a two-year cruise of the Pacific. He praised the islands as "Paradise" and later wrote in a *Cosmopolitan* magazine article in 1916, "Hawaii and the Hawaiians are a land and a people loving and lovable." His writings on Hawai'i are found mainly in *The Cruise of the "Snark"* (1911), a nonfiction narrative about his visits to Hawai'i and other Pacific Islands, and two collections of short stories, *House of Pride* (1912) and *On the Makaloa Mat* (1919).

Of his stories of Hawai'i, "Koolau the Leper" is perhaps the most famous. It is based on the story of Kaluaiko'olau, a 31-year-old Hawaiian of Kekaha, Kaua'i, who contracted leprosy, but resisted being sent to an isolation colony at Kalawao on Moloka'i for the afflicted. The segregation of people with leprosy began in 1873 under the Hawaiian Monarchy, but a group of about twenty-eight who had gathered in Kalalau, a relatively isolated valley on Kaua'i, was allowed to remain there until Sheriff Louis H. Stolz decided he would try to round them up. Stolz was an official of the haole-controlled Provisional Government (P.G.), which had replaced the Hawaiian Monarchy in 1893 after usurping political power and imprisoning Queen Lili'uokalani. When Stolz tried to arrest Kaluaiko'olau in 1893, Kaluaiko'olau shot and killed the sheriff and remained in Kalalau with his wife Pi'ilani and son Kaleimanu until his death, two years after the P.G. soldiers had given up trying to capture him. His son, who also contracted the disease, died shortly before him; his wife, who never contracted the disease (it was not as contagious as the Board of Health feared), remained in the valley alone for a year before returning to her family.

London may have heard the story of Kaluaiko'olau on his sail to Hawai'i on the *Snark*. One of his crew was Bert Stolz, the son of the sheriff whom Kaluaiko'olau had killed. London saw in the story a parable of Social Darwinism—the struggle for survival among individuals and races, with the fittest individual or race surviving, and the unfit doomed to extinction. He published "Koolau the Leper" in *House of Pride* in 1912. The story has remained alive in anthologies such as A. Grove Day's *Stories of Hawaii by Jack London* (1965, reprinted in 1990) and it is still used in schools, particularly in Hawai'i, by English teachers looking for "Hawaiian material" to assign to their students.

In "Memories of London" (*Honolulu Advertiser* 7 April 1993, C1+), Day, a former professor of English at the University of Hawai'i at Mānoa praises London as "a prominent writer about Hawaii....I have read him since childhood. He's one of the reasons I came to Hawaii, reading his stories." In the same article Scott Burlington, editor of a booklet on London's writings on Hawaiian surfing, announced his plan to erect a statue of London on Waikīkī beach. Burlington asserted that London should be memorialized because he "put surfing on the map" and his stories about Hawai'i describe "what Hawaii was" in the 19th century. I wrote a letter to the editor (*Honolulu Advertiser,* 18 April 1993, B3) opposing the plan because London's "Koolau the Leper" misrepresents Hawaiian culture and London was a racist. An English teacher at Kamehameha Schools, a school for children of Hawaiian ancestry, came to London's defense, arguing that London's intent was "to call attention to the plight of the oppressed" and that "a contrite Jack London...challenges his predominantly white audience to examine its own distant role in this dark segment of American history"—i.e., the "genocide" and "subjugation" of the kanaka maoli (*Honolulu Advertiser,* 2 May 1993, B4).

London's "Koolau the Leper" is a classic example of a work by a writer from a colonizing culture visiting a colony and usurping the voice of the indigenous people by telling their stories, imputing to the natives the world view of the colonizers and portraying the natives as accepting the fate of colonization. These narratives are then taught in the schools the colonizers establish, and inhabitants of the colony come to believe in the distortions and falsehoods. This practice continues today in Hawai'i's schools, public and private, from elementary schools to the colleges and universities.

Fortunately, Kaluaiko'olau's wife, Pi'ilani, gave her own account of the events, in her native language, to John G.M. Sheldon, who published it in 1906, as "The True Story [Mo'olelo 'oia'i'o] of Kaluaiko'olau," dedicated to Nā 'Ōiwi Hawai'i (the kanaka maoli). However, since for over half a century, the Territory and later the State of Hawai'i did not teach Hawaiian language in its educational system (for a while it was even banned from being spoken at school), relatively few people can read the Hawaiian version of Pi'ilani's story today. An English translation of the story, by Frances N. Frazier of Kaua'i, was published in *The Hawaiian Journal of History* in 1987. While Pi'ilani was a Christian, enough of the traditional Hawaiian world view remains in her account that a comparison of her story with London's reveals important differences between the values and beliefs of Euroamerican colonizers and those of the kanaka maoli.

London doesn't mention Koolau's ancestry and eliminates Koolau's wife and son from the story. He portrays Koolau in the American tradition of individualism—a lone hero fighting for his freedom. London's Koolau tells the captain of the soldiers who have come to capture him: "I am a free man...I have done no wrong. All I ask is to be left alone. I have lived free, and I shall die free. I will never give myself up." Later, the omniscient narrator comments, "Free he had lived, and free he was dying." Individual freedom is a basic value in London's American culture. London assumes, like other colonial writers and teachers, that his culturally specific values are "universal"; he attributes them to people he encounters in his travels. A would-be god, this author re-makes ("fictionalizes") everyone in his own image.

Pi'ilani begins her story with the names of Kaluaiko'olau's paternal and maternal grandparents (Kanemahuka and Keawe, Nakaula and Kawaluna) and parents (Kaleimanu and Kukui), and Pi'ilani's parents (Hoona and Kepola), as well as her own child, Kaleimanu. Kaluaiko'olau's identity was based on his family—ancestors and children—not his individuality. Pi'ilani reports that the motivation for Kaluaiko'olau's resistance to incarceration was not to maintain his individual freedom, but to keep his family intact: Kaluaiko'olau did not want to leave his wife alone on Kaua'i. He offered to go to Kalaupapa if his wife and son could go. When a deputy named Pokipala told him that the law prohibited anyone without the disease to live in the isolation colony, Kaluaiko'olau decided to resist arrest, and Pi'ilani supported her husband's decision:

> When this decision [to isolate people with leprosy on Moloka'i] was made known to Ko'olau, he directly said...that he was absolutely opposed and would not be taken alive to Kalawao [the land section next to Kalaupapa, where the original leper colony was located], unless his family could be taken too, and Pokipala departed to report this to his superior. My husband told me all this and we discussed what to do. And we agreed together to live patiently together in the hardships of this life, and that death only would separate us. (8)

Pi'ilani says Kaluaiko'olau was determined to stay together with her because of their Christian marriage vows:

> The consecrated law of marriage had come to us, and we swore by the holy book to live together in the time of food and of famine, in sickness and in health.... We swore to become one, never to leave one another, and now it is commanded that we be parted. The love that is implanted in my heart for my wife shall never be extinguished, and the oath I swore before God shall continue until I die. (13)

Deep and enduring attachment to one's spouse, which was valued in Hawaiian culture before Christianity, was reinforced by the modern oath of marriage. (Pukui notes, "The elders in my own 'ohana who mated *noho pū* ["to live together"], without contract or ceremony. And when the new laws came, they said, 'We don't need a paper marriage. We have always loved each other. We always will.' They knew about 'till death do us part,' but not because of *kauoha*, a command or a law. Because of what they truly felt" [Pukui et al *Nānā*, Vol. II,. 120].)

In London's world, the nature of the individual is to compete against and impose his will on other beings—humans, animals, and plants. As he lay dying, London's Koolau recalls his "lusty, whole-bodied youth," when he had the strength to dominate horses and bulls:

> As life faded and the drip of the rain grew dim in his ears, it seemed to him that he was once more in the thick of the horse-breaking with raw colts rearing and bucking under him, his stirrups tied together beneath him, or charging madly about the breaking corral and driving the helping cowboys over the rails. The next instant, and with seeming naturalness, he found himself pursuing the wild bulls of the upland pastures, roping them and leading them

down to the valleys. (362)

Koolau's will to dominate extends to Koolau's relationship with his fellow Hawaiians: Koolau is portrayed as the "king" of the group of resisters. He urges his followers to fight on with him and implies that they are cowards if they don't. He boasts that he could defeat a thousand soldiers by himself and promises salvation to those who are loyal to him. Like Jesus Christ, the king of Christians, Koolau is eventually betrayed by his followers after the cannon fire becomes too intense for them: "they preferred the prison of Molokai" to death. As the followers leave the valley, they "hurled imprecations and insults at Koolau as they went by; and the parting hag who brought up the rear halted, and with skinny, harpy-claws extended, shaking her snarling death's head from side to side, she laid a curse upon him." But London's individualistic hero doesn't need his follower; he fights on alone.

In contrast, Pi'ilani reports that Kaluaiko'olau's last thoughts were not about himself and his "lusty" youth, but about his family. He was particularly concerned for his wife's future and afraid she might be held responsible for the killing of the sheriff:

> Hear me, my wife, perhaps you have understood my troubles, since I know inwardly that I am weakening, and it is almost time for me to follow our child and leave you all alone, and how will it be with you?...We have lived together looking after each other, and when I go you must end your residence in this place and turn towards the homes of our families and give them all my love. Tell the truth if you are questioned, saying that mine was the trouble, which you and the child followed with me to the end, and that you fulfilled the oath you swore. (31-32)

Pi'ilani notes that one of Kaluaiko'olau's fears was that at Kalawao, which her husband calls "a strange land," his "bones would be laid without knowledge of the one who should attend to hiding his bones; whereas, here in the land of his birth [Kaua'i], I, his wife, would, he knew, lay him to rest forever" (13-14). It was important to Kaluaiko'olau that his family take care of his bones after his death and that he be buried in "the land of his birth," his 'āina hānau, so that no enemy would dig the bones up and desecrate them and so that his spirit, which lived on in his bones, and his mana (spiritual power) would remain near home to protect and assist his loved ones; even after death, he would be a part of his family's life.

Pi'ilani portrays her husband as a friend, not a "king," to other kanaka maoli. Instead of trying to persuade others to join him in resistance, he told them to leave the valley, so they wouldn't be harmed or killed:

> I shall not go back, I will remain alone, you all shall return [to the beach to be taken to Moloka'i]. For me alone is this death which is swiftly pursuing; your lives might be needlessly harmed; therefore my wish and command to you all, my people, is that you all return to the shore to avoid trouble. (19)

And later, when Kaluaiko'olau and his family were the only resisters left in the valley, Pi'ilani tells us that although her husband was suspicious of the people of the valley, the inhabitants were friendly and helpful to them. They occasionally provided food and supplies—"clothing, matches, and a bag of fish, dried moi, and some other things we lacked" (28). One man, Wili Kini, offered a cow. Kaluaiko'olau knew he couldn't repay the generosity of his friend, so he refused the offer. While historical evidence suggests that there was a mistrust between the residents of Kalalau and the refugees who had moved into the valley to escape internment at Kalawao, the $1000 reward which was offered for the capture of Kaluaiko'olau was never claimed.

In London's story, Kalalau Valley is a forbidding place:

> ...a flower-throttled gorge, with beetling cliffs and crags, from which floated the blattings of wild goats. On three sides the grim walls rose, festooned in fantastic draperies of tropic vegetation and pierced by cave entrances—the rocky lairs of Koolau's subjects. On the fourth side the earth fell away into a tremendous abyss, and, far below, could be seen the summits of lesser peaks and crags, at whose bases foamed and rumbled the Pacific surge. (351)

In this wild, untamed amphitheater of nature, the resisters struggle to survive because food is scarce and they are crippled by their disease: "The majority of them were too helpless to forage food for themselves under such forbidding circumstances, and all were starving. He [Koolau] selected two women and a man who were not too far gone with the disease, and sent them back to the gorge to bring up food and mats" (360).

In Pi'ilani's narrative, Kalalau is not wilderness; it was her family's protector and provider. Getting food was not a struggle for her family. Kalalau valley supported a large population in traditional times.

Archaeologist E. Craighill Handy writes: "It was one of the most intensively cultivated areas in the islands." Numerous terraces for planting taro lined the main stream. Even where the topography was "precipitous, rocky, and broken," the land was irrigated. "Every 10-foot square of suitable land was utilized. One small depression contains two terraces." By the end of the 19th century, of course, the Hawaiian population had been considerably reduced by diseases brought by colonizers and immigrants, of which leprosy was one; and farmers had deserted the remote valleys of Hawai'i for life in the city, so Kalalau was not as extensively populated and cultivated as it once was. Still, Pi'ilani tells us:

> The taro grew to the base of the pali and there was forest on either side. And there we were accustomed to take some taro and some luau, the green tops of the taro plants, and from the stream we got goby fish and fresh water shrimp and fresh water shellfish. There was hoio fern whose tender tips we ate, and with the fruits of the upland we had sufficient food and plenty of water to drink. We found this place had shelter and enough food for the welfare of our bodies, and we made this place into a home for ourselves. (26-27)

The land was alive, a sheltering parent:

> The sun above in the day, the dark clouds of Kāne at night, the rows of promontories was our world, the creeping, clustering leaves our ridgepole and shelter, the dew was our cloak in which we huddled.... When the sun descended into the sea in the west, and the wings of darkness spread over all the ridges of this place, it was awesome and lonely, but it was not long before the moon rose in its beauty and the moist breeze of the forest stroked us, and then the friendly voices of the land shells began to sound everywhere.... (21)

Pi'ilani expresses empathy for the suffering of the land under bombardment by cannon fire: "the P.G. soldiers continued to fire above Punee, and the earth and rocks of our little home flew about, and love welled up in us for the nest in which we had sheltered, because of its being needlessly harmed" (26). Later, after Kaluaiko'olau's death, the land snails sang out again, joining in Pi'ilani's lament. (These singing land snails are endemic to Hawai'i. The various species have names and epithets like pūpū kani oe, or "shell that sings continuously," or pololei kani kua mauna, "land snail singing from the mountain ridges"; Nathaniel B. Emerson says the sound was like the chirping of a cricket

(*Unwritten Literature* 121). The sound is apparently created by the vibrating of a membrane in the snail.)

In London's story, only one place name is mentioned—Kalalau Valley. Pi'ilani, on the other hand, in an uwe helu, or wailing chant recounting shared experiences with the deceased, remembers all the places that sustained and protected her family. Each place is given an epithet to humanize or personify it:

> Kamaile, "guardian of my husband"
> Kahalanui, "where we sheltered in our nest"
> Waimakemake, whose "sheltering foliage hid us"
> Koheo, "the friendly place which opened to hide us"
> Punee, "who saw the needs of hunger"
> Limamuku, "the place of refuge," where the family found ripening bananas
> Kalahau, "standing guard against the bullets"
> Oheoheiki, full of "abundance," where taro grew in a stream
> Kaluamoi, "the hospitable bosom"

This catalogue of place names is a traditional element of Hawaiian storytelling. For kama'āina (children of the land) place names are important as an expression of affection for the land which provides sustenance, and as essential reminders of the character and resources of each place. (Haole writers, like London, who re-tell Hawaiian stories often leave out place names; but readers familiar with traditional stories find such tellings uninformed because we expect specific details about the setting.)

Pi'ilani's narrative suggests three key values for human survival: Christian faith, knowledge of the land, and love and support from friends and family. As Kaluaiko'olau and his family hiked into Kalalau valley in the cold, driving rain (the cold was the main source of discomfort, not hunger), "Koolau removed his cloak, keeping only his shirt, and with loving hands he wrapped the child, showing his constant thoughtfulness and love for the child" (9).

In London's world, the highest value is individual freedom and the key to freedom is will. Each individual—or racial group—tries to impose its will on others; the one with the strongest will dominates and rules. London portrays Koolau as a hero because he believes Koolau's will to be free is stronger than everyone else's, including the collective will of the haole. In spite of his disease, Koolau is never captured.

London thought he recognized in Koolau a strong-willed, superior being like himself. But London did not view Hawaiians as a superior race that worshiped freedom and will like his own race. Koolau was an exception. In "The Lepers of Molokai," his account of his visit to Kalaupapa, London portrays the people in the colony as happy to be there:

> "They are so contented down there," Mr. Pinkham told me, "that you can't drive them away with a shot gun." This I later verified for myself. In January of this year, eleven of the lepers, on whom the disease, after having committed certain ravages, showed no further signs of activity, were brought back to Honolulu for reexamination. They were loath to come; and, on being asked whether or not they wanted to go free if found clean of leprosy, one and all answered, "Back to Molokai." (*The Cruise of the Snark*)

London's attitude is seemingly contradictory—he praises Koolau for fighting for his freedom; then praises the "lepers of Molokai" for accepting their incarceration; but the contradiction is only apparent. London isn't praising the lepers of Kalaupapa; he is justifying their incarceration. In his mind, the afflicted, mainly Hawaiians, were inferior beings who did not mind being imprisoned as long as all their needs were taken care of. His argument is similar to the argument used by Southern plantation owners to justify and romanticize slavery—the slaves enjoyed life on the plantation; they didn't mind being slaves because they were housed, clothed, and fed. They were inferior beings who did not want to be set free because they depended on their white owners to take care of them. London uses an "American negro" as an example of a former inmate of Moloka'i who would gladly return to the colony there. According to London, when the superintendent of the colony, Mr. Mcveigh, visited Honolulu, the Negro, a bootblack, begs to be sent back to Kalaupapa: "'Say, Boss, I lost a good home down there....Say, Boss, can't I go back? Can't you fix it for me so as I can go back?'"

If residents preferred living at Kalaupapa to living in the outside world, it was for more complex reasons than London was capable of discerning in them. Oddly, the English teacher at Kamehameha claims that London portrayed "the lepers of Molokai" with "humanity, vitality, and inner beauty" (*Honolulu Advertiser* 2 May 1993, B4).

In London's fantasy world, while Hawaiians and Negroes don't mind being imprisoned or enslaved, the "noble haole" cannot tolerate it. In another London story set in Hawai'i, "The Sheriff of Kona," a sheriff named Lyte Gregory, whose duty it is to send people with leprosy to

Kalaupapa, contracts leprosy himself and must be sent there. At first he accepts his fate—since he himself has sent so many to prison, he feels he should comply with the law. But he is not happy there, as the narrator explains: "'You see he was grieving about his wife and kids. He knew we were taking care of them, but it hurt him just the same.'" After nine months, a group of Gregory's friends carry out a bold rescue, and Gregory flees to Shanghai, where he lives as an anchorite, happy to be free, even though he is away from his beloved Kona and his family in Honolulu. Freedom at all cost.

London believed that love of freedom was the mark of a superior being, and Koolau was one of these superior beings. His irony is that while Koolau's will to be free is stronger than the haole's will to imprison him, Koolau is supposedly biologically weaker than the haole because he is susceptible to leprosy and other diseases. London was fascinated, and obsessed, by what he perceived as the subhuman state into which leprosy brought its victims:

> They were monsters—in face and form grotesque caricatures of everything human. They were hideously maimed and distorted, and had the seeming of creatures that had been racked in millenniums of hell. Their hands, when they possessed them, were like harpy-claws. Their faces were the misfits and slips, crushed and bruised by some mad god at play in the machinery of life. (351)

London's defender at Kamehameha Schools argues that London uses the diseased state as "a symbol for the genocide of the Hawaiians" (*Honolulu Star-Bulletin and Advertiser*, 2 May 1993, B4). What London actually believes is that disease is a sign of biological inferiority, marking a person as unfit for survival. On visiting the valley of Taipi sixty-five years after Melville, and finding the natives to be "wretched creatures, afflicted by leprosy, elephantiasis, and tuberculosis," London proclaims that "the Typeans crumpled up and went down before [various micro-organisms brought by white men]," then boasts:

> We of the white race are the survivors and the descendants of the thousands of generations of survivors in the war with the micro-organisms. Whenever one of us was born with a constitution peculiarly receptive to these minute enemies, such a one promptly died. Only those of us survived who could withstand them. We who are alive are the immune, the fit—the ones best constituted to live in a world of hostile micro-organisms. The poor Marquesans had undergone no such selection. They were not immune. And they, who

> had made a custom of eating their enemies, were now eaten by enemies so microscopic as to be invisible, and against whom no war of dart and javelin was possible. (qtd. in Sacks 225)

Toward the beginning of the story, London portrays Koolau railing against the haole for taking the land from the Hawaiians:

> Ours was the land, and behold, the land is not ours. What did the preachers of the world of god and the word of Rum give us for the land? Have you received one dollar, as much as one dollar, any one of you for the land? Yet it is theirs, and in return they tell us we can go to work on the land, their land, and that what we produce by our toil shall be theirs. Yet in the old days we did not have to work. (351-2)

This portrayal of Hawaiian protest against the overthrow of the monarchy and their dispossession of the land misrepresents Hawaiian culture: first London implies that kanaka maoli would not mind giving up their land if they had been paid for it; this reflects London's own capitalistic view of the world. The land in traditional culture was a living being, a parents, not a commodity to be bought and sold. Secondly, the suggestion that kanaka maoli did not work in "the old days" is ludicrous. They farmed and fished for a living; the work was more arduous than writing, which is what London did for a living. However, kanaka maoli did not have to work unceasingly, because they did not have the unlimited desire for wealth that motivates the capitalist.

In the end, London portrays Koolau accepting his defeat by the haole. This fictitious Koolau is made to admit that the kanaka maoli lost their land because the haole were more persistent and willful, and therefore more "fit to survive":

> Koolau forgot where he was, forgot everything, as he lay and marvelled at the strange persistence of the haoles who would have their will though the sky fell in. Aye, they would have their will over all men and all things, even though they died in getting it. He could not but admire them, too, what of that will in them that was stronger than life and that bent all things to their bidding. He was convinced of the hopelessness of his struggle. There was no gainsaying that terrible will of the haole. Though he killed a thousand, yet would they rise like the sands of the sea and come upon him, ever more and more. They never knew when they were beaten. That was their fault and their virtue. It was where *his own*

> *kind lacked* [italics added]. He could see, now, how the handful of the preachers of God and the preachers of rum had conquered the land. (360)

This passage epitomizes the strategy of colonization through the usurping of the native voice in storytelling. London inserts his own racist notions about the superiority of the white race into the thoughts of a fictitious Hawaiian; and at the same time, he makes Koolau deliver a requiem for his own people—the kanaka maoli were supposedly one of those populations, like indigenous peoples elsewhere, who were dying off and would soon be extinct because they lacked the will of the white man to persist. Koolau is a partial exception that proves the rule. Just as the sheriff of Kona is an exception, one of the few haoles who is susceptible to leprosy, Koolau is one of the few Hawaiians who "persists." Koolau continues to resists while the rest of his "kind" have given up. But he is only a partial exception, because he succumbs in the end to leprosy. He is not really a threat to white supremacy because he lacks immunity to microorganisms. In London's story, he dies, unable to reproduce himself.

The comments of Pi'ilani make it clear that Koolau and his wife held no such beliefs about the superiority of the haole. Judging others by their actions rather than their race, she is full of scorn for the boastfulness and cruelty of the haole soldiers, who have burned houses in the valley:

> They stupidly thought by this they would frighten and capture my husband. This was the wickedness and the worthlessness of these impertinent P.G. [Provisional Government] soldiers' actions toward the blameless ones and their houses and belongings ... my husband and I were filled with rage, and if perhaps we could have gotten some of them we would have wrung their bones and fed them to the fire. Until this day I am not done brooding over these plundering, burning, thieving P.G. kōlea, the birds who come to fatten on our land, who came as wanderers and arrogantly lived on the sweet breast of our native land. [The kōlea, or golden plover, flies south from Alaska to spend the winter in Hawai'i, growing fat here, then returns to Alaska to nest in the summer.] (22)

Pi'ilani attributes the loss of the land not to Hawaiian lack of will, but to the greed and ruthlessness of the newcomers. London would probably agree that the haole were immoral, but in his belief system, what matters is who wins.

Far different from London's Koolau, the Kaluaiko'olau that Pi'ilani portrays was not a lonely individualist who valued only his personal freedom in rebelling against the government authorities; Kaluaiko'olau was a loving husband and father, who refused to leave his wife and son alone on Kaua'i and whose wish was for them to bury him in the sands of his birth and to care for his bones. He valued his 'ohana (family) and his 'āina (the land that nourishes and provides for one), not his personal freedom. Kaluaiko'olau was Hawaiian, not American.

Some of the differences between London's and Pi'ilani's stories can be attributed to London's desire to make the story more "dramatic." He adds more episodes of violent confrontation and death than actually occurred. He was writing fiction, of course, not history or autobiography. Yet the boundary between fiction and non-fiction is really not that distinct. Fiction often melts into fact in the reader's mind; and what appears to be fact is often fiction. Words create virtual realities. The issue in comparing these two versions of the story of Kaluaiko'olau is not that London's story is fiction, and therefore false, and Pi'ilani's is autobiographical, and therefore true; Pi'ilani had her motives for telling the story, one of which may have been to avoid prosecution for any of the events that took place in the valley. That she feared such prosecution, she admits. It was one reason why she stayed in Kalalau for over a year after her husband died.

At issue is what effect reading London's "Koolau the Leper" in isolation might have on student readers. Because teachers and students in Hawai'i have so little knowledge about the indigenous culture, it would not be too far-fetched to fear that a reader of London might believe, as Scott Burlington seems to, that London describes 19th century Hawai'i "as it really was," or that (as London's wife believed) London knew Hawaiians "better than any one." If we read his stories with these assumptions, we would believe that the kanaka maoli valued individual will and domination; that they didn't mind incarceration as long as they were housed and fed; that they didn't work before the haole came; that they were biologically inferior to the haole because they lacked immunity to certain diseases; that they admired the haole for his persistence. These beliefs are far from the truth. Whether anyone can describe historical experience "as it really was" is questionable, but one would get far closer to the reality of Hawaiians in the 19th century by reading native Hawaiian writers like Pi'ilani than by reading London. What one learns from London is how colonial writers think and perceive others.

The assumptions of London's story—that survival depends on imposing one's will on others and that might makes right—are downright detrimental to the survival of a island community. We need to teach young people better values than that.

Afterword

On May 2, 1997, I visited the famous land of Kalaupapa for the first time. The voyaging canoe *Hōkūle'a* left Mānele Bay, Lāna'i, at 4 a.m, the crew mainly college students learning the arts of voyaging. We were towed across the 'Au'au Channel before the wind came up, to Līpoa Point on Maui; then sailed on a beam reach across the Pailolo Channel and downwind along the north shore of Moloka'i to Kalaupapa. The plan was to stay there a couple of days, before returning to Honolulu.

As we left Mānele, a dim glow in the clouds covering the southeastern slope of Haleakalā grew very bright, as if the clouds were burning and this dormant volcano were going to erupt; then the mountain gave birth to a cradle of light, which rose slowly into the predawn sky—Kāloakūlua, the 25th moon, a day when the kapu for Kanaloa, an ocean god, was freed; a day of calm seas, "a good day for planting crops"; "a good day for the birth signs of men..." (Kepelino 110)

The north shore of Moloka'i was spectacular, vertical basalt cliffs dropping straight down into the sea and deep green valleys, once populated, now deserted. Even this isolated coastline, with no modern development or roads, was filled with stories. We sailed past Kikipua, where a mo'o woman of that name was slain by Hi'iaka, Pele's sister, on her way from Maui to O'ahu (Emerson *Pele and Hi'iaka* 83-85); past Wailau where 'Ai'ai had punished the people for their wanton fishing by taking away all the 'ōpae and 'o'opu, restoring them to the high waterfall on the cliff of Koki, as a favor to his favorite, Kahiwa, a local lad (Manu 22-23); past Hā'upu, the site of the famous fortress of Kape'epe'ekauila, a Moloka'i ali'i who conducted raids from there against foreign chiefs from the South Pacific (Kalākaua 69-94; cf. Summers *Moloka'i* 208-211); we stopped to greet Joyce Kainoa at her house, a solitary pioneering effort on a steep ridge above Hā'upu Bay; then on past Anapuhi, the cave which had been the home of the puhi who raided Kū'ula-kai's fishpond in Hāna, Māui, and who was slain by 'Ai'ai, its backbone turning into stone at Leho'ula (Summers *Moloka'i* 184-185; Manu 2); we sailed through the narrow gap between Leina o Papio ("Papio's Leap"; Summers *Moloka'i* 185-186) and the island called 'Ōkala ("Bristling"); past Waikolu, where the prophet Hulumaniani stood looking east up the coast we had just sailed down and saw a rainbow over a ridge at Malelewa'a at Wailau, where the the princess

Lā'ieikawai was hiding.

By 4 p.m., we were anchored off Kalaupapa Settlement. The scattered buildings and houses had the look of the World War II Era and reminded me of the small rural towns of Hawai'i in the 50's. Sixty or so aging residents are still living at Kalaupapa, along with a support staff. The settlement has been designated as a National Park, but the residents are permitted to live there as long as they want to.

On the afternoon of our second day there, a couple of the residents came up to the porch of the old wooden dormitory where we were staying to talk story. First, 84-year old Aunty Sarah, a relative to one of the crew members. She had burns on her arms from a coffee pot, which her damaged fingers had trouble grasping. Still, she was lively and loved to hug. She recalled appreciatively the visit of a hula halau—how the dancers performed a dance in honor of a place called Nihoa, on a shelf of land beneath the tall cliffs just west of Kalaupapa, where a pig was said to have rooted into the hillside, causing a landslide. This narrow piece of land, 2,700 feet long and 1,000 feet at its widest, can be reached only by a rocky coastal trail; it has its own wind, the Makakuapo (Summers, *Molokai* 196), and is famous for its fragrant hala trees ("Nā hala o Nihoa, he māpuana la"; Emerson, *Unwritten Literature* 203). Aunty Sarah also remembered caves on the Peninsula that some Hawaiian families used to live in before they were removed to make way for the Settlement. Her niece was taking notes, hoping one day to write Aunty Sarah's story.

The oldest resident, 87-year old Kenzo Seki, came walking up the steps announcing that he had heard "the *Hōkūle'a* gang wanted to see me." Born in Hilo in 1910, he was diagnosed with Hansen's disease when he was 10 and sent from Honolulu to the old settlement at Kalawao in 1928; he later moved to the new settlement at Kalaupapa. He had a 1928 truck parked in his front yard up the street. Like Aunty Sarah, he loved to play: "People thought you could get sick if I touched you," he would say, then grab your arm and laugh. Another of his favorite sayings: "I didn't come here, I was sent here." He recalled that they used to fish by throwing dynamite onto the reef. (How would 'Ai'ai have punished that "wanton" method of fishing?) After he left, we saw him pass the porch driving a pick-up truck at about 5 miles an hour, his fingerless hands grasping the steering wheel, his head barely visible above the door.

What struck me about the two residents was that they were ordinary people, not the symbols of the subhuman or the biologically inferior that London had created through his lurid descriptions and gross stereotypes—absurd products of his overheated fancy. Aunty Sarah and

Kenzo had contracted a disfiguring disease and were forced into isolation by a terrified community. They, along with others with Hansen's Disease, had endured, forming their own community on this separate piece of land beneath the high cliffs of Kalaupapa. Decades passed; the terror subsided. Free to go now, they had decided to live their lives out here, in a place which had become home.

Kenzo passed away from a stroke in 1998. His obituary in the *Honolulu Advertiser* (25 August B1+) lists the bare facts of his life: baptized a Catholic, he became a lay minister. He started a Boy Scout troop and took young girls on camping trips as well. He was a founder and leader of the Kalaupapa Lions Club. He invented devices that could be used by those with impaired hands to button a shirt and open a beer can. He left instructions that his body not be sent to Honolulu; he wanted to remain in Kalaupapa.

Glossary

'ahi: albacore, or yellow-fin tuna; trolled for with hook and line; in season from May to August; 'ono; eaten raw, baked, or dried.

āholehole: a perch-like fish, 6-10 inches long; silvery gray on top, whitish below; found near shore living in lava or coral caves (lua); 'ono; eaten raw, dried, salted, or broiled on hot coals.

'āina: land; lit. "that which feeds" a person.

ahupua'a: land division extending from uplands to sea.

aku: bonito, or skipjack tuna; 2-3 feet long; caught using a pā, or pearl shell lure; considered the most 'ono fish by some; every part was eaten, from head to tail, raw, dried, or baked.

akua: god, spirit, or goblin.

ali'i: chief; a person having a noble bloodline.

'anae: mullet; 8-12 inches long; found near shore and in brackish water; known for seasonal migrations; netted near shore or raised in fishponds; eaten raw or cooked.

'aumakua, 'aumākua (plural form): family god.

'auwai: irrigation ditch.

awa: milkfish.

'awa: a shrub; an intoxicating, medicinal drink is made from the root.

'elepaio: a native bird; species of flycatcher.

hala: pandanus tree; the leaves were used for weaving baskets and mats.

hāpu'u: grouper, or sea bass, a deep water bottom fish, about two feed long.

hau: a type of hibiscus; its light wood was used for net floats and canoe parts; the bark was twisted into a strong rope.

he'e: octopus, from small reef ones to large deep-water ones (up to 6-7 feet long).

***heiau*:** a temple; a place to worship the gods.

***hīna'i*:** a basket trap; various sizes and kinds were used to catch various kinds of fish.

***hīnālea*:** a wrasse; predominantly dark blue, green, or black, with sometimes colorful markings; 3-10 inches long; lives on reefs; caught with a basket trap; eaten raw or cooked.

***honu*:** sea turtle.

***Ho'oilo*:** the cooler, wetter season from October to April; cf. Kau.

***imu*:** underground oven; food was placed in a pit with hot rocks and buried until cooked; a person might be put to death by being baked in an imu; his flesh could then easily be stripped from the bones.

***ipu*:** gourd.

***kāhala*:** amberjack, six or more feet long; silvery blue with yellow stripe along each side; taken with hook and line; eaten baked or salted.

***kahu*:** caretaker.

kahuna*, *kāhuna (plural form): a priest or an expert in any art or profession.

***kai*:** sea.

***kala*:** surgeonfish with a horn on its forehead; named for the seaweed on which it feeds (limu kala); 12-24 inches long; taken in baskets or nets, or speared; it has a strong odor, but is well liked; eaten broiled, baked, or dried.

***kalo*:** the taro plant.

***kama'āina*:** native-born or long-time resident; lit., "child of the land."

***kanaka maoli*:** native people; lit., "true or real person."

***kapa*:** tapa cloth made from tree bark.

***kapu*:** law, rule, prohibition.

***Kau*:** the hotter, less rainy season from April to October; cf. Ho'oilo.

***kī*:** the ti plant.

***kīhei*:** a piece of bark-cloth worn over the shoulder.

kinolau: a physical form (plant, animal, or natural phenomenon) taken on by a supernatural being.

koa: a native hardwood tree.

ko'a, or ***ko'a kū'ula***: a shrine sacred to a fishing gods, offerings were placed on it to attract fish, make fish multiply, and insure a good catch; the altar was a large stone or two, sometimes on a paved platform; or a heap of stones and coral rock near shore.

ko'a (also *ko'a i'a*, or *ko'a lawai'a*): fishing grounds.

kona: the lands on or direction toward the leeward side of islands, away from the prevailing ENE trade winds; usually the drier areas on an island because the clouds brought by the trade winds are blocked by the mountains; cf. ko'olau.

konohiki: the person who managed an ahupua'a for a ruling chief.

ko'olau: the lands on and direction toward the windward side of islands, facing the prevailing ENE trade winds; usually the rainiest areas on an island because the clouds brought by the trade winds turn into rain as they rise over the mountains; cf. kona.

kūmū: goatfish; 5-16 inches long; found in both shallow and deep water; 'ono; eaten raw, broiled, or cooked in ti leaves; often used as a religious offering if a red fish was needed.

kūpīpī: a grayish reef fish, palm-size, with a black spot near its tail; 'ono, raw, cooked in kī leaves, or broiled; also dried.

kū'ula: a house or shrine dedicated to a fishing god; also a stone used to attract fish. The house was where the fishermen slept before going fishing for certain fish, such as the 'ōpelu; the men worshiped the fishing god and purified themselves with a ceremony (see Malo 209-210), and sometimes sought visions of schools of fish or of the outcome of the expedition; the men were forbidden to go home and sleep with their wives.

lau hala: leaves of the hala tree; used to weave baskets and mats.

limu kala: a seaweed on which the kala, or surgeon fish, feeds on; it was used to bait basket traps to catch kala.

līpoa: brown seaweed, branching, with blade-like leaves; highly prized as food.

lo'i: pond fields for growing wetland kalo.

lunawai: "water master" in charge of distributing water from an 'auwai or stream.

mahimahi: dolphin fish.

maka'āinana: common people, cf. ali'i, or nobility; lit. "people who attend to the land"; the word is a cognate of Marquesan-Tahitian mata'eina'a, meaning "land-owning descent group."

mana: supernatural power.

mamo: a pale reef fish with black stripes, palm-size; 'ono raw or broiled.

manini: a striped surgeonfish; 3-5 inches long; a common, popular reef fish; 'ono, raw or cooked.

makai: toward the sea; cf. mauka.

mauka: toward the mountains; or toward land, if one is offshore; cf. makai.

manō: shark.

moano: a reddish goatfish, 6-12 inches long; caught on reefs or in the deeper water just off the reefs; 'ono, raw or broiled in kī leaves.

moi: threadfish; 18 or more inches long; tawny yellow with light brown stripes; 'ono, raw, dried, or broiled in kī leaves; formerly not common; reserved for the ali'i, or chiefs; today it is grown on sea farms.

mō'ī: king.

mo'o: a supernatural water lizard.

'ohana: family; extended family.

'ōhi'a 'ai: the mountain apple tree; lit. "edible 'ōhi'a"; its flowers resemble the flowers of the 'ōhi'a lehua tree, but are whitish; the red fruit is juicy and sweet.

'ōhi'a lehua: native tree with red flowers of spiky, thin petals.

'ō'io: bonefish; 2-3 feet long; silvery; travels in schools; caught with nets just inside or outside the reef or breakers; 'ono, raw or mixed with limu.

olonā: a native shrub; the bark was made into a strong durable line for fishing or nets, or for lashing together houses and canoes.

'omaka: a herring (makiawa), 3-10 inches long; 'ono, raw, salted, dried, or baked.

ono: a large mackerel; a wahoo.

'ono: delicious; to savor.

'o'opu: gobey fish.

'ōpae: fresh or salt-water shrimp; the freshwater ones were caught in mountain streams with a basket woven from the air roots of the 'ie'ie (a woody branching climber).

'ōpakapaka: blue snapper; a deep-sea bottom fish; better liked by haole than by the kanaka maoli; Kepelino says the fish is "fleshy but insipid."

'ōpelu: mackerel scad; 12 inches long; dark blue fading to white on belly; netted in deep water; 'ono; eaten raw, dried, or broiled.

pā: mother-of-pearl shell; pearl-shell lure; pā hī aku: pearl-shell lure for catching aku.

pāpio: the young ulua.

po'opa'a: "hard head," a hawkfish, found on reefs; easily caught; some eat it, but not highly esteemed by fishermen.

pua 'i'i: tiny fish fry.

pueo: the Hawaiian owl.

puhi: eel.

uhu: parrot fish; 1-3 feet long; red or green; found along the shores of all the islands; abundant from May to July; caught with hook and line, in a reef trap, or with a net using a live decoy attached to a string to lure the fish in; 'ono; the flesh sometimes eaten dried or broiled, but preferred raw, especially the red variety, mixed with its mashed liver and seaweed.

uku: grey snapper; a deep-sea bottom dweller; grows up to 3 feet; 'ono.

ula: lobster.

'ula'ula: red snapper; a deep-sea bottom fish; 17-30 inches long; red or rose, with yellow or golden bands extending along upper half of body; 'ono, eaten raw, dried, or broiled.

***ulua*:** crevalle; up to five feet long and weighing 100-125 pounds; light and dark varieties; caught with hook and line in deep water; eaten raw, baked, or broiled. "The eyes were well liked; stuffed into the belly before the fish was placed in the imu."

***'u'u*:** a red squirrel fish, with large eyes; 'ono, raw or broiled; called menpachi by local Japanese fishermen.

***wauke*:** the paper mulberry; its bark was made into kapa cloth.

***weke, weke'ula*:** goat fish, red goat fish; 9-14 inches; taken near shore; 'ono when broiled in ti leaves.

Bibliography

Abbott, Isabella Aiona. *Lā'au Hawai'i: Traditional Hawaiian Uses of Plants*. Honolulu: Bishop Museum, 1992

Ancient O'ahu: Stories from Thrum and Fornander. Honolulu: Kalamakū Press, 1996.

Andrews, Lorrin. *Dictionary of the Hawaiian Language*. Rutland, Vermont: Tuttle, 1974. (First published in 1865.)

Arens, W. *The Man Eating Myth: Anthropology and Anthropophagy*. Oxford: Oxford University Press, 1979.

Beckwith, Martha. *Hawaiian Mythology*. Honolulu: UH Press, 1970. (First published in 1940 by Yale University Press.)

Beckwith, Martha. *The Hawaiian Romance of Laieikawai*. Translation of *Laieikawai* by S.N. Hale'ole. Washington D.C.: Government Printing Office, 1919. 285-666.

_____. "Hawaiian Shark 'Aumākua." *American Anthropologist*, Vol. 19, No. 4 (Oct.-Dec. 1917): 503-517. (Reprinted in Emma M. Nakuina et al. *Nanaue the Sharkman and Other Hawaiian Shark Stories*. Honolulu: Kalamakū Press, 1994.)

Buck, Peter. *Vikings of the Pacific*. Chicago: U of Chicago Press, 1938.

Bushnell, O.A. *The Gifts of Civilization: Germs and Genocide in Hawai'i*. Honolulu: UH Press, 1993.

Chun, Malcolm Nāea. *Nā Kukui Pio 'Ole: The Inextinguishable Torches: The Biographies of Three Early Native Hawaiian Scholars Davida Malo, S.N. Hale'ole and S.M. Kamakau*. Honolulu: First People's Production, 1993.

Cleghorn, Paul. *Prehistoric Cultural Resources and Management Plan for Nihoa and Necker Island*, Hawai'i. Honolulu: Bishop Museum, 1987.

Devaney, Dennis M., Marion Kelly, Polly Jae Lee, and Lee S. Motteler. *Kāne'ohe: A History of Change*. Honolulu: The Bess Press, 1982.

Emerson, Nathaniel B. *Pele and Hiiaka: A Myth from Hawaii*. Honolulu: 'Ai Pōhaku Press, 1993. (First published in 1915.)

_____. *Unwritten Literature of Hawaii: The Sacred Songs of the Hula.* Rutland, Vermont: Tuttle, 1965. (First published in 1909 by Bureau of American Ethnology.)

Emory, Kenneth P. *Archaeology of Nihoa and Necker Islands.* Honolulu: Bishop Museum, 1928.

Finney, Ben. *Hōkūle'a: The Way to Tahiti* . New York; Dodd, Mead, 1979.

_____. *Voyage of Rediscovery: A Cultural Odyssey Through Polynesia.* Berkeley: UC Press, 1994.

Fornander, Abraham. *Ancient History of the Hawaiian People.* Honolulu: Mutual Publishing, 1996. (Volume 2 of the three volume *An Account of the Polynesian Race,* published from 1878-1885.)

_____. *Collection of Hawaiian Antiquities and Folklore,* Vol. 4, 5, 6. Edited by Thomas G. Thrum. Honolulu: Bishop Museum, 1916-1920.

Frazier, Frances N., Translator "The True Story of Kaluaiko'olau, or Ko'olau the Leper" (Originally published in Hawaiian in 1906 by Pi'ilani, wife of Kaluaiko'olau.) *The Hawaiian Journal of History.* Honolulu: Hawaiian Historical Society, Volume 21 (1987): 1-41.

Fujimura, Faith N. and Williamson B.C. Chang. *Groundwater in Hawai'i: A Century of Progress.* Honolulu: UH Mānoa, Water Resources Research Institute, 1981.

Green, Laura, and Mary Kawena Pukui. *The Legend of Kawelo and Other Hawaiian Folk Tales.* Honolulu, 1936. (On Microfilm 1534. No. 2, Hamilton Library, UH Mānoa.)

Gutmanis, June. *Na Pule Kahiko: Ancient Hawaiian Prayers.* Honolulu: Editions Limited. 1983.

Hale'ole, S.N. *The Hawaiian Romance of Laieikawai.* Hawaiian text with English trans. by Martha Warren Beckwith. Washington: Government Printing Office, 1919.

Handy, E.S. Craighill. *History and Culture of the Society Islands.* Honolulu: Bishop Museum, 1930.

_____. *Polynesian Religion.* Honolulu: Bishop Museum, 1927.

Handy, E.S. Craighill and Elizabeth Green Handy, with Mary Kawena Pukui. *Native Planters in Old Hawaii: Their Life, Lore, and Environment.* Honolulu: Bishop Museum, 1972.

Handy, E.S. Craighill, and Mary Kawena Pukui. *The Polynesian Family System in Ka'-u Hawai'i.* Rutland, Vt: Tuttle, 1972. (First published in 1958 by the Polynesian Society, Wellington, New Zealand.)

Hawaiian Drum Dance Chants: Sounds of Power in Time (Compact Disk with Liner Notes). Washington, D.C.: Smithsonian Folkways, 1989.

Henry, Teuira. *Ancient Tahiti.* Honolulu: Bishop Museum, 1928.

Henry, Teuira, et al. *Voyaging Chiefs of Havai'i.* Honolulu: Kalamakū Press, 1992.

Ii ['I'i], John Papa. *Fragments of Hawaiian History.* Honolulu: Bishop Museum, 1959.

Johnson, Rubellite Kawena, and John Kaipo Mahelona. *Nā Inoa Hōkū: A Catalogue of Hawaiian and Pacific Star Names.* Honolulu: Topgallant Press, 1975.

Kahananui, Dorothy M. Ed. and Trans. *Ka Mooolelo Hawaii.* Honolulu: University of Hawaii, 1984.

Kalākaua, David. *The Legends and Myths of Hawaii.* Rutland, Vermont: Tuttle, 1972. (First published in 1888.)

Kamakau, Samuel M. *Ruling Chiefs of Hawaii.* Trans. by Mary Kawena Pukui et al. Honolulu: Kamehameha Schools, 1961.

_____. *Ka Po'e Kahiko / The People of Old.* Trans. by Mary Kawena Pukui. Honolulu: Bishop Museum, 1964.

_____. *Tales and Traditions of the People of Old / Nā Mo'olelo a ka Po'e Kahiko.* Trans. by Mary Kawena Pukui. Honolulu: Bishop Museum, 1991.

_____. *The Works of the People of Old / Na Hana a ka Po'e Kahiko.* Trans. by Mary Kawena Pukui. Honolulu: Bishop Museum, 1976.

Kame'eleihiwa, Lilikalā. *A Legendary Tradition of Kamapua'a, The Hawaiian Pig God.* Translated from *Ka Leo o Ka Lāhui.* Honolulu: Bishop Museum Press, 1996.

_____. *Native Land and Foreign Desires.* Honolulu: Bishop Museum Press, 1992.

Kāne, Herb Kawanui, "The Seekers" *Mānoa: A Journal of International Writings.* Vol. 5, No. 1 (Summer 1993): 15-23.

Kepelino, Keauokalani. *Kepelino's Traditions of Hawaii.* Translated and edited by Martha Warren Beckwith. Honolulu: Bishop Museum, 1932. (Reprinted in 1978.)

Kikuchi, William K. "Prehistoric Hawaiian Fishponds" in *Science,* 23 July 1976: 295-299.

Kirch, Patrick. *Feathered Gods and Fishhooks: An Introduction to Hawaiian Archaeology and Prehistory.* Honolulu: University of Hawaii Press, 1985.

Kyselka, Will. *An Ocean in Mind.* Honolulu: University of Hawaii Press, 1987.

Landgraf, Anne Kapulani. Nā Wahi Pana o Koʻolaupoko: Legendary Places of Koʻolaupoko. Honolulu: University of Hawaii Press, 1994.

Leib, Amos P. and A. Grove Day. *Hawaiian Legends in English: An Annotated Bibliography,* 2nd Edition. Honolulu: UH Press: 1979.

Lewis, David. *We the Navigators.* Honolulu: University of Hawaii Press: 1972.

London, Jack. *The Short Stories of Jack London.* New York: Macmillan, 1990.

_____. *The Cruise of the Snark.* New York: Macmillan, 1911.

Lyons, Paul. "From Man-Eaters to Spam-Eaters: Literary Tourism and the Discourse of Cannibalism from Herman Melville to Paul Theroux." *Arizona Quarterly,* Vol. 51, No. 2 (Summer 1995): 33-62.

McAllister, J. Gilbert. *Archaeology of Oahu.* Honolulu: Bishop Museum, 1933.

Malo, David. *Hawaiian Antiquities.* Trans. by Dr. Nathaniel B. Emerson. 2nd Edition. Honolulu: Bishop Museum, 1951. (First published in 1903.)

Malo, Davida. *Moolelo Hawaii.* Edited by Malcolm Nāea Chun. Honolulu: Folk Press, 1987.

Manu, Moke et al. *Hawaiian Fishing Traditions.* Honolulu: Kalamakū Press, 1992.

Melville, Herman. *Typee.* New York: Penguin / Signet Classic. 1964. (First published in 1846.)

Montaigne, Michel de. *Complete Essays.* Trans. by Donald M. Frame. Stanford: Stanford UP, 1958.

Munro, George C. *Birds of Hawaii.* Rutland, Vermont: Tuttle. 1960. (First published in 1944.)

Nakuina, Emma M. "Ancient Hawaiian Water Rights And Some of the Customs Pertaining to Them." *Hawaiian Annual* 1894: 79-84.

Nakuina, Emma M. *Hawaii Its People, Their Legends.* Honolulu: Hawaii Promotion Committee, 1904.

Nakuina, Emma M. et al. *Nanaue the Sharkman and Other Hawaiian Shark Stories.* Honolulu: Kalamakū Press, 1994.

Nakuina, Moses K. *Moolelo Hawaii o Pakaa a me Ku-a-Pakaa* Honolulu, 1902. (Reprinted in 1991 by Kalamakū Press)

_____. *The Wind Gourd of La'amaomao.* Trans. by Esther T. Mookini and Sarah Nākoa. Honolulu: Kalamakū Press, 1990. (Re-edited and reprinted in 1992.)

Noyes, Martha. "Cultural Abuse." *Honolulu Magazine,* November 1996: 36+.

Parfit, Michael. "Diminishing Returns: Exploiting the Ocean's Bounty." *National Geographic.* November 1995: 2-37.

Polynesian Voyaging Society WWW Site (http://leahi.kcc.hawaii.edu/org/pvs)

Pukui [Pūku'i], Mary Kawena. "Canoe Making and Descriptions." A translation of "Kalai Waa Ana a Me Kona Mau Ano" by Z.P.K KawaikaumaiiKamakaokaopua (Kalokuokamaile), published in *Nupepa Kuokoa,* October 26-1922-February 15, 1923. Manuscript in Bishop Museum.

Pukui, Mary Kawena. *'Ōlelo No'eau: Hawaiian Proverbs and Poetical Sayings.* Honolulu: Bishop Museum, 1983.

Pukui, Mary Kawena and Samuel Elbert, *Hawaiian Dictionary.* Honolulu, UH Press: 1986.

Pukui, Mary Kawena, Samuel Elbert, and Esther Mookini. *Place Names of Hawaii.* Honolulu, UH Press: 1974.

Pukui, Mary Kawena, with Laura C.S. Green. *Folktales of Hawai'i / He Mau Ka'ao Hawai'i.* Honolulu: Bishop Museum, 1995. (A compilation of stories first published in three separate volume in 1923, 1926, and 1928.)

Pukui, Mary Kawena, E.W. Haertig, M.D. and Catherine A. Lee. *Nānā I Ke Kumu (Look to the Source),* Vol. I and II. Honolulu: Hui Hānai: 1972.

Pukui, Mary Kawena, and Alfons L. Korn. *The Echo of Our Song: Chants and Poems of the Hawaiians.* Honolulu: UH Press: 1973.

Rice, William Hyde. *Hawaiian Legends.* Honolulu: Bishop Museum, 1923.

Sacks, Oliver. *The Island of the Color Blind.* New York: Vintage Books, 1996.

Stannard, David. *Before the Horror: The Population of Hawai'i on the Eve of Western Contact.* Honolulu: SSRI. 1989.

Summers, Catherine C. *Hawaiian Fishponds.* Honolulu: Bishop Museum, 1964.

_____. *Molokai: A Site Survey.* Honolulu: Bishop Museum, 1971.

Sterling, Elspeth P. *Sites of Maui.* Honolulu: Bishop Museum, 1998.

Sterling, Elspeth P., and Catherine C. Summers. *Sites of Oahu.* Honolulu: Bishop Museum, 1978.

Tava, Reitorerai, and Moses K. Keale Sr. *Niihau: The Traditions of an Hawaiian Island.* Honolulu: Mutual Publishing, 1989.

Thrum, Thomas G. *Hawaiian Almanac and Annual.* (also called *The Hawaiian Annual.* and *Thrum's Annual*) 1875 - 1932.

_____. *Hawaiian Folk Tales; a Collection of Native Legends.* Chicago: A.C. McClurg and Co., 1907.

_____. *More Hawaiian Folk Tales; a Collection of Native Legends and Traditions.* Chicago, 1923.

Titcomb, Margaret. *Native Use of Fish in Hawaii.* Honolulu: UH Press, 1972. (First published in 1952 as Memoir 29 of the Polynesian Society, Wellington, New Zealand.)